Tuning the Blues to Gold

SoundPrints

Vickie Dodd

[signature: Vickie Dodd]

WovenWord Press

Cover art: Marilyn Punahele
Cover design: © 1999 Traci Schalow
Cover photo: Eric Neurath

ISBN 0-9658137-1-1

Library of Congress Catalog Card Number
99-70961
Tuning the Blues to Gold: SoundPrints
Dodd, Vickie
Includes compact disk
Healing through sound

WovenWord Press

TABLE OF CONTENTS

ACKNOWLEDGEMENTS

My greatest gratitude goes to the thousands of men and women that trusted and allowed me to sing their bodies' songs. They taught me their ways of being alive so that I could eventually be taught our own common song. For this I am eternally grateful.

Many thanks and blessings go to the following people who contributed their time and energy to this project and to my work. I want to thank Pat A. Paulson for "finding" the book and for the many hours she spent helping me to see it. Heartfelt thanks to Kay Gardner who has consistently supported and encouraged this work and who kept saying, "just get the book out, Vickie." I am thankful for the vision of Diana Somerville, Alana Shaw, Norah Haldeman, and Mary Capone who revealed the book's form and function. A special thanks to all my students of the Anatomy of Sound School that helped ground this work so that it could be de-mystified and communicated. Also, a special acknowledgement to Mark McCoin of Brave New Audio, for generously contributing his expertise and many hours of studio and editing time, and then starting all over again! The book was blessed by the energies of Mary Gaul, Nancy VanArsdall, Marilyn Punahele, Zoe Keithley, Diane Hennum, Robyn Sullivan, and Lynn Daniels, who read the book, blessed it, and said, "yes, go ahead." I needed all of their juices, and I am so fortunate for such a strong, loving community. The ultimate fruition of this book was brought about by WovenWord publishers Sheila Dierks and Vicki McVey. They walked me through the steps of publishing and made it workable and exciting. Vicki McVey, my editor, very gently eased me through the process of simplifying what most needed to be communicated. Finally, much gratitude to Eric Neurath, my partner, who kept me and the project rooted in the earth with his relaxed, calm appreciation of "just do the next thing."

Mainly I thank Source and the Muse that creates us all.

A Living Book

I first met Vickie Dodd in Chicago in 1981 when she gave me the gift of a sound treatment. I remember it as being one of the most transforming experiences of my life, though at the time I intellectualized it. I was amazed at how I felt after an hour and a half of her sounding the emotional pain and anguish embedded in my tissue, spiralling those sounds into harmonics (overtones) and then into the healing hum. I remember that I climbed off her table feeling that all of the molecules in all of my cells had been rearranged and reorganized.

Over the years of our friendship and association as colleagues in the field of sound healing, Vickie has asked me to make sounds with her, but I've been either too repressed, embarrassed, or too attached to my own emotional denial to do it. While reading *Tuning the Blues to Gold: SoundPrints* aloud, as it *must* be read, my sounds were given permission to flow. At a certain point in the book (it may vary for each reader), I felt myself open. My tears began to flow, and release began. As I read on, I felt my heart open more and more and my voice grow stronger and more resonant with each sound print.

This book is revolutionary. Because it's predominantly in verse, it is rhythmic and has meter. Be prepared to laugh. Be prepared to weep, to cry, to sob, to whine, to moan, to groan. Be prepared to heal. Be prepared to remember your source, to loose the bonds of denial, to know who you really are. Be prepared to read aloud, to sound aloud, to take the sounds deep into your cellular memory where Mother-Father Source reside.

> This book opened me
> This book opened me
> This book opened me to my pain
> This book opened me to my gain
> I want to read it again and again
> To help me feel
> To help me steal my soul back
> 	from denial
> Ah ta anna oh
> Ah ta anna oh
> Ah ta anna oh

Kay Gardner,
February 9, 1999

THE LIVING BOOK

I am so grateful for the direct experience that matter can be changed with intention, prayer and a resting-assured that all is possible and that mystery lives and is simple and uncomplicated. This experience sustained me for many, many years when there wasn't any support for frequency healing, and later when interest became great in the "alternative" world but such experiences were only acknowledged if they occurred in other cultures. I could rest assured knowing that Spirit and Mystery and Wisdom did not belong to only a few, that no group had a monopoly on God, and that if we went far enough back into any and all our lineages we would find the simple ways of Earth Wisdom that existed before we created such great complexities and separateness.

A Living Book

This book is about the work I have done for the past thirty years. I want to tell of the intricacies, complexities, formulas of sound frequencies that I meet with daily. I had planned on writing it as a scientist and as a mathematician, but as I began to write, the words came out in cadences, in the rhythms of their aliveness.

This book is a living book. This book is to be read aloud; it is an experiential reading. The sound of your voice will help resonate the sounds behind the words to touch your body and deepen your experience. This book is written for your body, not your head. It is written for the physical, emotional, psychological and spiritual bodies. It is written in these variety of rhythms so that the words may be able to drop in and penetrate the bodies. It is written so that the stories may touch the commonalty of our histories and help us begin to feel, begin to move, begin to remember, begin to accept, begin to connect, begin to foster courage, begin to see the thread of the various imprints. Your stories may be of a different flavor or hue, but I trust that you will find a thread of familiarity that cannot be overlooked, especially if you encourage your willingness to keep looking.

I wrote this book so that the sounds could be within the words; that the impact of the words could enter the body; that the body would stir the memories of the feelings that the sound and rhythm of the words ignite.

This book is written as a way to create acceptance for that which may be unexpressed bodily. This book is written to release the body of past stored memories, so that the body can become current, present, conscious, neutral, to go toward it's birthright, it's evolutionary intelligence, it's future.

The pieces in this book have been designed and placed to foster an experience of following a thread, a fiber of denied rhythmic expression throughout the body. Acceptance and willingness to stay in the journey are necessary to fully transform the blues into gold. By feeling the dissonance and following it, it will move and guide you to a place of understanding, to a place of transforming the memories to present time, to current time, to neutral time, to a place of grace with no hooks to the past. For in a place of neutral, there is freedom for movement and the possibility for evolution.

Carl Jung says that if you find the psychic wound in an individual or a people, there you will also find their path to consciousness. For it is in healing of our psychic wounds that we come to know ourselves.

SoundPrints

This book demonstrates a spiral layering of the physical anatomy of the emotional body. I have translated the sounds I have perceived in peoples' bodies into words. The SoundPrints and the Spiral exercises placed throughout the reading are to be read out loud in your own phonetic interpretation. The exercises are a demonstration of one possibility of expression. They are presented to encourage you to interpret what you perceive. You would not "hear" how I "hear," nor "sound" as I would "sound." You would "hear" and "sound" through your own interpretation. There is not a right way for them to be read. Your own voice has the ability to be more accurate for your body than another's voice. Initially, others voices assist us to find our own. The SoundPrints are placed here to assist you, the reader, not just to integrate the words more fully physically, emotionally, and psychologically, but also to experience the power of sound as a transformative tool. The Spiral exercises are designed to unwind held patterns of conditioned thinking and conditioned feelings in our bodies. This book unwinds spirally, a layer of denied expression, recorded stories of our blues, our anger, our guilt, rooted in our Mother God and Father God issues, our grieving turning us to prayer: prayer for surrender and the grace of acceptance of our humanness.

All of the exercises and SoundPrints in the book reference their location on the accompanying CD by track number. The track number is located on the page containing the specific exercise or SoundPrint. The exercises and SoundPrints have been recorded in the order they appear in the book, but due to the limitation on total track numbers available on a CD, several are grouped together on each track. Therefore, you may have to search through several exercises to find the one you want.

TAPPING THE LINEAGE (Track1)

I was born into a cultural pocket
                that fed me a current
that I could not deny.

It showed itself simply;
It showed itself crudely;

      It showed itself the only way
          that it knew how
       as it didn't know any other ways.

It was out-of-the-current, of the antennas
              that gave views
            of how other's lived.

It was not hooked-up and televised.

It was spent . . .
     It was plenty . . .

It gave me privacy
     It gave me time
         to not forget.
Before I had begun.

The women were what I listened to
         from the vantage place
      of underneath our kitchen table.

Listening to them was a rhythm of chorus and bugling
         and streaming forth caricatures of
             time.

Being born into a cultural pocket that was not included in the prospering industry of
post-war times;
        Eldorado had been missed.
     You could get your hair done at 25 cents a head in my Mom's kitchen.

You could have your eyes read,
Your dreams interpreted,
The sex of your unborn child disclosed . . .
                just for the
                time it took to bobby-pin
                someone's hair and
                comb-out
                              another.

      And if the time was right . . .
      maybe get a tap dance thrown in . . .

      As I was always willing and ready to tap a few rhythms that ran through all
the life that I listened to . . .

      And, I listened plenty . . .
          I heard plenty from the pulses of life that all
humanity is made up of . . . to the pulses of life of the
Earth and the plants and the rocks and the stars.

This was my symphony. This was my Soundscape; and of course
it included all the anger, concerns, jealousies, disappointments,
lust-felt "stuff" floating in any bodies' air.

   Denial wasn't a word then
      but, that didn't stop it from
         happening.

So, my Mom got me some tap shoes and I tapped the rhythms of what I heard and
felt. And other's seemed to enjoy listening and watching me.
 And, I felt so fluid,
         listening and tapping . . .
         it was a complete circuitry.
         What came in, got expressed creatively
         in the percussive steps.

I even got to dance in several mental hospitals, tapping out the emotional, mental, physical states of some of the members in the audience.

IT WAS THE SOUNDPRINTS

Audibly producing the inaudible message. And, it was such a gift for all of us.

The rhythms didn't get stuck or housed in me and others got their rhythms expressed.

I am grateful that we were not all sitting around watching television . . . as my tapping would have probably been disturbing!

I remember the sound of the rocking back and forth of the wringer washing machine. I loved the groove it kept time to and then the sloshing of the water and the agitator doing the in-between notes of the bassline.
This was my favorite bassline to tap
between and over and even do melodies that floated up from
the steam and smells of laundry.

I never tired of this rhythm . . . even today I can hear it:

Shalum shaluk
shalum shaluk
shalum shaluk
shoosha lo
shoosha lo
shalum shaluk
shalum shaluk
shoosha lo
shoosha lo
shalum shaluk

Ms. Haley made me beautiful costumes, black satin with black-net blousy sleeves, red and white satin with sequins . . .

I tap-danced all over Southern Illinois and Missouri and Kentucky. It was the first sound school I attended and taught at the same time.

> It showed it's light on me
> It shed it's veils
> It gifted me by giving me
>   a pallet to express the unexpressed.

> I was a player of the drum with my feet,
> The earth was my drum skin,
> The composition was it's inhabitants
> The arrangement was Grace . . .

I am grateful for never having needed to question the mystery.

As I reflect on my rural childhood community, I note that they were practicing their own forms of natural healing which I later came to recognize as iridology, herbology, neural-linguistic programming and massage. They lived in the knowing of the natural order of life. Again, I have much gratitude that I was born at a time in a geographic pocket that still had memory and respect for "common sense."

Thank you, Grandma

My earliest memories of women as healers began around the kitchen table, as the women in the area would meet at my folk's house to have my Mom bobby-pin their hair, and to smoke their corn cob pipes and chew their tobacca, (as there were few places where that was an acceptable act), and they would talk and gossip.

They lived their lives a lot according to their dreams. They always seemed to know when someone was pregnant and if it was going to be an easy or difficult birth; they said they could tell by their eyes . . . we now call this iridology, I'm sure. Their dreams would tell them when someone was going to die, and I remember my Grandma grieving when her husband got killed in a major mine disaster and her telling about begging him not to go as she knew he wouldn't be coming back. But, by those years, these dreams and feelings weren't listened to, they were referred to as "old wives tales." And now, nearly 40 years later, myself and many others are embracing the "old ways."
Sometimes acting like we created them. . . .

I remember going with my Grandma and Mother to pick wild greens and herbs, digging sassafras root every spring to clean our blood after the heavier foods consumed in the winter. There was much common sense wisdom that was there all around me and it has taken me full circle around to thank these people for still being alive and keeping their ways, at least for a little while when I was young. My greatest direct experience with the abilities was with a woman called Grandma Baggott. For one year I had a wart growing inside my mouth, on the underside of my lip. We had been going to this Doctor in town for nearly a year, once a week, for various treatments, to burn it off. Nothing was getting it. Our last visit to Dr. John he told us we'd have to go to a town 80 miles away to the hospital, to have it surgically removed. We were walking home from his office and met Grandma Baggott at the main corner, and my Mom told her what was happening with me. She said "let me see that, honey." I pulled my lip out and showed Grandma Baggott this big wart, and she put her hand on my shoulder and said "You won't have that tomorrow." And . . . I didn't. It was gone the next day when I awakened and never re-occurred. Thank you Grandma.   1985

Gifts Of The Journey

At seventeen I left home and began my search for how my understanding of sound could be of service to the world. I had also been told in a "sonic" vision, a loud voice that had been with me since childhood, that I needed to learn how the emotions lived in the physical body, and that this knowledge would be crucial for my own well-being. The emotional bodies of the people around me were audible to me. I was like a sponge for their denied or suppressed emotions. Without boundaries, I couldn't determine where other's emotions stopped and where mine began. Needless to say, I was in a considerable amount of pain. It became clear that in order to survive I had to learn how to transform these feelings. I followed this quest with the fiery passion of my youth.

The next several years, I studied many disciplines. I was on a mission to learn as much as I could about how the physical body housed the emotions, and about sound, light, and color. Much of this information I wove into my practice not knowing where one discipline started and the other ended. Several of these learning experiences are worth noting.

In 1970, I met Dr. Rammurti Mishra and began studying Sanskrit and acupuncture at his Ashram in Monroe, New York. Dr. Mishra was a Brahman, a Sanskrit scholar, and prior to my meeting him had been a psychiatrist and neurosurgeon at Bellevue Hospital in New York. He was a truly remarkable teacher who influenced me greatly. Daily, he taught us Sanskrit grammar *kri d ati, kri d atah, kri d anti*, as I massaged his feet up to his knees. Up until then, I had no way of discerning one body system from another. What I did hear was a conglomeration, an orchestration of many rhythms, pulses, fluids, musculature, and the weaving of the emotional stories, injuries and memories all living and swimming together in the physical body. But as I massaged Dr. Mishra's well-tuned body, I was able to concentrate on one meridian at a time. All other sound disappeared. Just the frequency of one single meridian presented itself as I followed its pathway and positioning through the body. As I continued this daily massage, Dr. Mishra's body taught me how to start listening with distinction, how to perceive any imbalance along the flow of a meridian. This was monumental. It marked the beginning of my ability to discern one bodily system from another. From that moment on I spent the next decade exploring my own body, using it as a laboratory to learn to distinguish organs, and the endocrine, glandular, and circulatory systems and their various rhythms and impulses. The chakra systems, the emotional imprints within the organic function, became my passion.

Several years later, I met another inspiring teacher, William David, aka Elias DeMohan, who founded the first school of sound, color and vibration in the United States, in Houston, Texas. Besides learning about sound and color therapy, William David helped me to reclaim my voice. Although I'd always been able to perceive frequencies from living matter, my own voice was weak and strained. I'd even been diagnosed with throat nodules as a teenager. This condition was not caused by over use, but from not expressing what I perceived. It was then that I began to truly appreciate how difficult it was for people to use their voice, especially for emotional, physical or spiritual expression. I recognized the courage it took to open this creative expression center. Under William David's guidance, I was able to discover for myself the pleasure, joy, and satisfaction that the reclaiming of my voice could bring. He gave me tools that I use to this day to teach others using breath, vowels and consonants to integrate the emotional and mental bodies.

Within months of meeting Elias, I met and started studying with Judith Aston, creator of Aston-Patterning. Her training aided me immensely in being able to match physically what I could perceive energetically and audibly. What I wanted when I first met Judith, was to have my outside reflect my inside, and she said, "I think that can be arranged." And that is what occurred . . . an integrity and authenticity of my beingness. Judith gave me a framework for describing and expressing my inner knowingness. Each of these teachers gifted me with acceptance of how I was and the confidence of who I could grow to be. I am most fortunate and grateful for their participation and support.

THE AUDIBLE BODY

Introduction of the HUM
(Track 2)

Say your name out loud
(your speaking voice)
repeat your name over and over
as if you are gargling mouthwash
let your gargling soften and turn into a hum.

The Audible Body

For the past 30 years, I have maintained a practice as a teacher, counselor and body worker using the medium of sound. I have worked with thousands of people listening to their bodies, not what their mind says about how their bodies feel, but how their bodies speak from their own experience. What I have learned from consciously listening is that our commonalties weave our common thread. Most of us think that our abuse experience is our uniqueness, that our personal story or history is what makes and keeps us different. Actually the opposite is true. Our stories and our histories are what makes us the same. Our uniqueness is expressed in how we survived, how we kept our humanity, and what we have created with what we were given. It is not our story that makes us special. It is our creativity that gives us our distinction.

Through this work I have observed that we all experience some degree of body-mind amnesia. Through my work, I have noted a substance that resides in the body. It is something I have felt vibrationally from almost every client I have worked on. It is a mucilaginous substance, a sticky liquid that covers and surrounds the nervous system, embedding itself into the brain stem. It covers the "feed" lines to the electrical system of the body. It coagulates causing the pulsation of currents in the body to become more faint, making it more difficult for the upper brain to sense the needs of the lower brain, the body. The bodily system becomes more susceptible to dehydration. The experience of it seems to be the absence of rhythm, pulse. I don't know what causes this or if it was always there. I do know that it manifests as amnesia in the body, suppressing the memory terminals in the brain. It coagulates in such ways that it almost becomes a separate life in itself, living within the physical body. It keeps us from remembering who we are, what we're up to. It makes us forget that the most important work in our lives is to become conscious.

All teachers that I have heard speak about "conscious awakening" agree that one needs to do some form of work every day to achieve this awakening. I have found that sound helps to dissolve, melt, change the structure of the body to become more fluid, transforming this coagulation into protoplasm which allows hydration to occur. When I speak of sound, I do not separate out sound, light, color and movement. Although they can be broken down individually, in my experience, they are the same, translating as different octaves or vibrations of each other. Sound breaks up crystallization. Sound creates a resonance so that movement starts to manifest and the reverberation continues.

Sound is a definitive tool for the inner terrain of the physical body, a conduit which is 80 percent fluid with an electrical current running through it as the generator. Sound work is dynamic in nature. It always creates change. When we are exploring our inner bodily terrains, our bodily laboratories, we want to notice where there is pulse and rhythm and where there isn't. Where there is rhythm we match its resonance and then follow the pathway it takes us on, and where there isn't we can use sound to begin awakening the numbness to discover its unique pattern of rhythm.

The "hum," a method and exercise referred to often in this book, provides the strong foundational work that enables us to engage this substance and our amnesia. Practiced daily, the hum softens and keeps the passageways throughout the body liquid. The "hum" employs consonant sounds, allowing it to resonate in the body, creating a reverberation and massaging the inner landscape.

For this method to work, consistency is a major component. It is in the process of doing, tracking and noticing what occurs that we start learning how sound works within us. Using ourselves as a laboratory allows us to learn this first hand. I spent many years on a daily basis using sound, "humming" into a place of numbness, amnesia, before I felt a small movement, a reverberation, an awakening begin to happen. By using the "hum" I started waking up the sleep, waking up the deadness, waking up the rhythm that was denied expression.

The physical body is a wonderful ground to do the work of awakening, for there isn't any separation of the emotional, spiritual, physical or psychological bodies. Just like color, light and sound, these bodies are different layers, hues or patterns of the same system.

The physical can be touched. My intention with the use of sound and light is to unravel, to make liquid the old paradigm of the physical body influencing the posture, central nervous system, belief systems, thought forms and the myriad of possibilities where denial lives. Wherever denial lives in the physical, mental, emotional or spiritual bodies, it shapes itself to the dimension in which it resides. In the physical body, it appears as the coagulation of substance, often lacking rhythm or pulse, that I've discussed earlier. In the emotional body, it manifests as stuck, repetitive responses. In the mental body, it shows itself as vicious circular thinking. In both the mental and emotional bodies there is a characteristic limitation of rhythms and pulses that are acceptable, so the range is narrow and often we refer to this way of being as a familiar path or groove or rut.

This denied expression keeps us busy always trying to fix something, to maintain the status quo, sometimes referred to as sanity, or to alleviate pain through maintenance therapy. Trying to live a transformational life, without having the willingness to acknowledge the placement of denial or amnesia in our lives, usually means living a high maintenance life. We never get much past the next fix. Trying to fix ourselves with all of our knowingness can be a very stressful lifestyle, requiring constant vigilance, no rest. Always more to do . . . the absence of Grace and Compassion.

I really don't know if it is possible to erase or awaken denial completely, or if that is even a goal. I do know that the process of expressing denial, giving it voice, movement, light, vision, form, creates a possibility for neutral. Neutral is a place of detachment, an opportunity to unhook from the past, a place of possibility to accept the unknown. The acceptance of the unknown is an opportunity for Compassion: Compassion for our Humanness, Compassion for our human frailties, Compassion for our imperfections. Self Compassion becomes the key to stepping away from, stepping back from the recorded repetitive responses, a place of rest and Grace. Resting Assured allows the receptivity of other rhythms, pulses, messages that are out of our usual groove or loop.

Sound Makes Us Honest

Sound makes us honest. We do not know what sound is doing, going to do, or what it can do. Each sound reveals another possibility.

Sound is an audible print of our contents, our stories, our histories, our interpretations of all that has happened to us. Our bodies have recorded these audible prints throughout our limbic system, nervous system, tissue, and cellular structure. Patterns of denial held in the body attract complimentary frequencies, sympathetic resonances. Patterns get embedded and entrained into the neural pathways, keeping us repeating the same behavior. In other words, "insanity is doing the same thing the same way and expecting different results."

When we change the frequency and pattern of rhythms, we start changing the form. All matter is held together with sound, light and color frequencies. The body is held in its shape by frequency. Our tissue, the energy fields around us, radiate these frequencies and reflect our feelings and emotions. Sound can increase or decrease the vibrancy of the frequencies. All is quickened or slowed down.

The effect is an audible painting of rhythmic color. Sound is an art, a skill that transforms discord into accord, dissonance into resonance, imbalance into balance.

IT'S A THREAD (Track 2)

It's a thread, you're saying . . .

It's a thread you're saying . . . It's a thread that can make all
       the difference, a thread pulled here,
            can loosen the entire garment.
       The entire fabric of time.

It's a thread you say . . . that's all I need to know?
      A thread to pull,
        a thread to tighten
      a thread to re-arrange . . .
   That's all I need to know . . . to do . . .
        to weave
    the past and the present and the future?

That's what you're saying?
      That it's a thread?
    That if I remember the Future
      the Present will be different and the Past is for sure changed?

Now, let's see . . . you're saying . . . it's only a thread . . .

And, that trying to change the present, always seems hopeless . . .
    as the present doesn't look much different than the past.

And, you mean to say, it's only a thread
      pulled or tucked,
        snipped and shifted
         and angled . . .
   That could change the future.
And it would be easier than going back to go forward;
   and, I'd just go forward and change the back
           as in past.

Even though, although,
you know they're the same . . .
past, present and future. But, since you know . . .
    I think of them as different timings;
    you're giving me the timing to begin to think the same.
And, you say, that since I know how I want life to be . . .
        and I know how life has been . . .
        and, I even suggest I know how it is . . .
Then it's all pretty simple.

        Remember the future
            in the way you wanted the past
       and it can become the present.

So, I need to become a weaver, you say.
I need to be a mender-of-sorts . . .
      actually sort-a-lot
Go into my netting and my gridwork
and start looking for any tears, openings, rips, apertures in the fabric . . .
               it's only threads.

Take my gold and silver needles and hooks and start weaving and crocheting and
sewing the fabric of my life.
If one thread is changed in a fabric, the whole entire gridwork is rearranged . . .
        Is that not true you say?

You say . . . It doesn't matter what I have to do . . .
How busy I am and all the folks that need my time and my wares.

The only thing I've got to do is to get my time straight of what's true.
Whatever I'm up to doesn't count, if I'm not using my time to get myself, you say?

It's a thread, you're saying . . .

WAKING UP THE AMNESIA OF WELLNESS

There is a cell that lives within us
that truly remembers wholeness,
that has recorded in itself
our inherent wisdom
of how to live in wellness;
how to live healthy
and how to live in contentment.
For years and years we have all been teaching and hearing and reading
that wherever we put our attention
is what we create.
And I have noticed with myself and others
that most of the attention
of our going toward wholeness
is through looking at what is not whole,
what is not ready and willing,
what is not yet done.

There seems to be a huge belief system
that runs us, generally speaking,
stating that healing cannot take place,
that full health is not possible.
Denial uplifted, expressed, exposed is to be applauded.
It takes so much energy,
so much good work,
and so much processing to reveal ourselves to ourselves,
to piece together the missing links
so that we can become more aware
having light shone upon our patterns
and paths of behavior.

But since we tend to think linearly, we just keep digging and digging.
Yes, we want to be good children
and note our every blemish
and its lingering scar and effect.
This way of being lacks MERCY, GRACE and COMPASSION;
the absence of NATURE,
the absence of the NATURAL ORDER and blueprint of healing, the SPIRAL.
There isn't any end or closure, linearly-traced.
Suffering on this planet, recorded molecularly, is infinite.
Once we note, acknowledge, express, feel, amend, and see our wound and the
path our wound has woven in our system, then we know the infinite story of ages
and ages, and everyone else's as well.

I do not wish to trash my past, or anyone else's, but I wish to start looking for another placement of self-looking-at-self. I would go through a layer at a time, and keep
going back and finding another thread to weave, even though I noticed that I found
the same story on each layer, differentiated only by its placement.
I am beginning to wonder (as the Zen koan speaks about) if
one can become one with anything, one can become
one with all.
In other words, once we have become one with our path of
healing on one layer,
maybe we can actually start toward a movement of evolution.

We've worked so hard and endured so much
to become whole,
to become one,
to become enlightened, enlivened.
If we are able to perceive one layer
the pathway of one layer;
then it is not necessary
to keep going back
and finding another

One layer fully tread,
        Gives one all the information, input
        on how that same path, thread,
           is interfaced through
              all the systems.

We need only to acknowledge that
        we have healed, uncovered,
           recovered our pathway
              of dis-content.

Then we can be able to start evolving
        to do the work ahead
          to be on the path
            of THE WAY AHEAD.

I wish to speak to that cell that remembers; to speak to it in its own language, in its own rhythm, that it may pulsate and vibrate to move and spread itself through more cells, more dimensions, and start a revolution, an evolution, a call to awaken.

WAKE UP, WAKE UP
        Hello in there
           Are you alone in there?
           Are you home in there?

WAKE UP, WAKE UP
        And listen to me
           I need you to see
           You make a difference to me.

I'm going to AH you
I'm going to CALL you
I'm going to do whatever it takes
        to make you ALL me.

I know that once upon a time
    to be blind
       was sublime
    was the way to survive.

WAKE UP, WAKE UP
I'm not saying it's too late
    or that it's even your fate
I'm just wondering if you're tired
    of having to fake
    That you're not AWAKE?

I can hear you singing joyfully,
I can feel you hugging yourself
I can smell your senses as you exude
    sweet thoughts to you and yours.
I know you are in there, whole and well.

And, I know for so long, you've
    been afraid I'd tell
       that we are truly well
that we do love ourselves
    that we are fine
        and couldn't complain
          about a thing.
But, now, what would all the others think?

That we are for sure
       in blind denial?
        delusion?
          idealistic?
       for sure not facing reality.

The habit is great to be sick.
> The support is there, if you please:
> I make my living on this disease.
> Why and how could I displease
> so many
> by my release
> of sleep?

My greatest fear is that you will
> know I am well
And will not need me any more
will not feed me any more.

My greatest fear is that I am
> well, and I can not
> find anyone else to admit
> that they are also.

The risk of being well
> is the warrior of the future.
> is the belly warrior,
> is the heart warrior,
> is the will to see Well.

One little cell is all it takes
> to change and re-arrange
> one's entire fate,
one's entire notion
> and quotient
> within the vast ocean
> Of Self.

SOUND SESSIONS

*Acceptance of
what is . . .
is probably the
most important
ingredient
for
Evolution*

SOUND PERMISSION SESSION

We are here to express all
of our emotions
The goal is not to make the
right note
but to make the sound that
is in the rough.
Just as a crystal of the mineral
kingdom
Must go through the experience of
opening,
Our sounds come from a raw
state
Before they become beautiful
glowing, polished
tones.
We use our sounds to polish
the stone.

Being willing to make the
sound that is now
not who you will be . . .
not who you would be . . .
if things were different.

Give Voice
Movement
Expression
as you
Read

Feel where you
Feel

STORYTELLING SESSION

The Sounds are telling
    stories,
        telling histories,
            telling tales
                of Archetypal
                    forms
                old as the
                    origin of
                        time.

Speak the words with sound
    Sound gives it movement
        Movement de-personalizes
           Movement gets the
                mind out of
                  the way of
                    the words.

As you read, feel where
    the story lives in
        you
When you feel, make the
        sound/feeling.
    If you get scared
        sound your scared
    if you feel mad
        sound your mad
    if you feel
        rest
sound your best.

Mainly keep breathing
 keep moving, as
  the story not
   fully told
    leaves one
     incomplete
     or not
      in tune.

So, if all the characters
  created by being
   alive
  get to be voiced
   in their uniqueness
   then each can
    be sung
     together
   as a whole.

This Book is a connection
of words and sounds.
This Book is a collection
of Collective Consciousness.

These are just some of our stories
  Some of our words
   that are in sounds
  of a human life

These words are a collection
    of sounds, almost
        Archetypal stories
        I have heard
        in people's bodies
            over the years.
They are designed
    to unravel a layer
      of denial
    A layer of discontent
      A layer of holding.

They are designed as a spiral
    Unfolding and reclaiming
        dimension as
           its story gets
              spoken
      as the veil gets
        lifted
As the trust becomes
    such
that we know if
    we give to that
      which is unsaid
    we need not live by
"that which is unexpressed runs the show."
Sounds of words used
    in this book
      are for the
transformation of
    the words
      in the body.

These are stories:
>of the Past
>of the Future
>Archetypal
>what happened
>someone else's story
>Collective Consciousness
>of the Present
>>all the many concerns

And what happens in the overlay
>>and the underlay
>and the in-between layer
>of the at-randomness
>>of interplay
>called:
>Blockages
>Stuckness
>Resistance
>Congestion

Introduction to The Whine

(Track 3)

Find your Hum

Let your little girl or boy voice come out, kind of nasally sound,

and COMPLAIN! BITCH! MOAN!

about whatever is running through your mind; as example:

"I don't understand what she's asking. I don't know how to do it,

I'm afraid that it's not right, I'm tired right now, I can't, no one

understands me,

I don't have time, I don't feel good . . . they don't like me, I can't stand them.."

(No more than 10-15 seconds).

With your nasal voice let the words start being all mixed up

as if in a blender or centrifuge

spin the words into sounds,

spin sounds into your HUM.

SPIRAL WHINE
(Track 3)

nnnn oooo uuuu HMM
oooo HMM HMM HMM
nnnn I'm afraid I'm lonely, HMM
oooo AH I don't do it HM
HMM AH it right I'm UH
hummmmm AWH I good enough, No one understands, I'm lonely, UU
hmm uH not UH UH
wwwwwwwwwmmmmm uH UH AW AW AW No one URR URR
UH URR URR URR

That Which is Unexpressed Runs the Show

WE ARE PIONEERS

I know that by voicing the unspeakable
it gives permission and
acceptance of that which is yet unknown.

Acceptance of how we are embryos of what sound is
going to
effect
in our world.
We are pioneers.

WE SOUND TO GET TO QUIET

Much of the reason
to give voice
and expression
to all the many
and varied characters
is so that we may
become quiet
and silent enough
to be able to
listen

Chaotic Sound Exercise To Get Quiet
(Track 3)

Listening to the conversation you are having in your head
RIGHT NOW
the dialog you are having NOW
the ONE you are nearly always having,
even when you are having other conversations
and don't even remember
or NOTICE that there are several "conversations"
going on . . .
just follow your mind for a moment . . .
or follow the "story" or "stories"
that you find yourself telling over and over
everywhere.
This is what I want you to sound, voice, express
instead of trying to get them to settle down, give them a voice, their voice, your voice.
BE OUTRAGEOUS
start with the words of the story,
then let the words become sounds
then let the sounds spin and spiral into your hum.
Do this daily for a while or whenever needed to get quiet enough to listen. (no more
than 5 minutes)

A SOUND SESSION

"Sounds"' many ways

As many times
    the Sounds are words
      that cannot be spoken.

Cannot be spoken because
    there are too many words
    all crowded together
    interfaced . . . sandwiched
    by a variety of experiences.

The Sounds of words contain
      content of one's life
      context of one's life
      and archetypal characters
               in life.

The Sounds contain all
    the truth that
    didn't get told
All the secrets that
    had to be kept

The words get stuck
    in the Body, not
      just the head.

A Sounding Session
    is being a storyteller.

The first Sound sessions
    start differentiating the
      various stories

Start unraveling
    the holding patterns
      that take place
        just because
          there was
            an opening,
              a bruise,
              an injury,
              for the taking.
Start unraveling the
    "stuff" we might
  have gotten
      because our boundaries
        are loose,
      because we're human,
        because at-randomness
    may exist
Maybe just because. . . .
The Session Starts unraveling
    the content
      that has already been
        "cleared,"
        "understood," "processed,"
          "Amended,"
But is still in the tissue.

Sounding these Various worlds of Words
    begins to create
      discernment.

A Storyteller
    of this world of words
      would take six to eight people
        telling their story
          at the same time.

Relax, Ground
Yourself
One needs much
Grounding to
Receive and
to
Remember
that you
Received

Grounding Exercise
(Track 3)

Sit comfortably, feet flat on the floor.
Remind yourself that the chair you are sitting on can and will support all of your weight, all of your thinking and feeling.
Put your attention at your pelvis, specifically your coccyx (tailbone).
Image a grounding rod, a tube going down into the earth extending from your coccyx. Let your rod have earth colors, black, brown, reds, and have the rod go 1-2 miles into the earth.
From the place in the earth, the rod separates into 2 rods and returns from the earth to the arches of your feet.
This earth energy now comes into your feet, into your legs, into your genitals and belly and back down your grounding rod into the earth, from the earth back up into your feet, legs, belly, back down into the earth. Establish and continue this rhythm.
While you are doing that, put your attention about 1 foot above your head and see and feel a blue-gold color of cosmic energy coming through your crown center, into your head, filling your head and neck, going along both sides of your spine, filling your chest and back and meeting at your coccyx, joining with the earth energy.
Like a centrifuge, the earth source and the cosmic source spin and mix and dance together. Together they spiral up the spine, through the head, chest, back, belly, buttocks, legs;
some of the cosmic energy goes down the grounding rod into the earth.
It is a dance.
Close by starting the spiral dance at the lower spine and spinning up the spine all the way through the head, through the crown, and letting the energy fountain out of the crown center and rain and spout forth and cleanse the front, back and sides of you down to your feet. When this feels complete, bring your attention back to your grounding rod, review and ground. When that feels rooted for you, gently rock forward and softly shake your hands of any excess energy and give thanks for your life.

A SOUND SESSION (CONTINUED)

Sound creates discernment.
   Sound creates a clarity
      for knowing
       what's my story
not just the many
     words that
         got tangled up
           and created
      their own
          entity.

So in a Sounding Session
   You give each story
     its sound, its emotion
     its rhythm,
        its timing,
          its cadences
   So that it has its
       own shape,
its own geometry.

The Story or Stories
   are actually shaped
     by the various
       formulas
         or placement
           in our systems.

They may not
      be personal.
Please, as you read
   give yourself room
      to have a different
        story
   if you cannot find
     yourself in the one being
         told.
See if the emotion or
     rhythm
Touches one of
      your own
Or maybe one of a
       Loved one.

Silent Hum

IMAGINE
(with your mind's eye)
saying your name
repeating it over and over
feeling it and "seeing" it spin inside your head
like a gyroscope,
letting the spin of your name turn into a hum.
Imagine your hum
spiraling and curving inside your body
introducing you to your interior landscape.
Your HUM is a MASSAGE
moving you and touching you.

Guide your sound into your chest and back,
your belly, your legs,
see your sound embrace your shape and form.
Your sound spirals inside you,
touching your inner terrain.
Remember you are a 3-dimensional body,
a front, a back and sides.
You can make sounds silently
that you probably could
never make aloud.
Our range becomes unlimited.
The entire interior is our domain
and is accessible.
We start being able to sense our
unique orchestration.

THE ART FORM OF SOUND DISCERNMENT
AS A PARADIGM CHANGE

This art form is a
   beginning way to unravel
   the old paradigm in
      our body's posture, stance,
      nervous system, belief
      systems and thought forms.
The art of releasing
   denial on all levels
   of our beings, to
   be willing to move and
   mature the feeling,
   emotional body.
The art form for
   going toward a
   new paradigm,
   a new vision
   of self and others.

Every part gets a voice

The head says one thing:

The belly another:

The heart another:

They each speak
        and mix and match
           each other
           in a place
           of meeting
A place of permission
    for their own experience
      of truth.

We should be able to do this and stay centered.

Does it really matter that we do this?

I'm holding on as much as I can . . . I'll survive!

41

Sound is Food
for the System,
It dissolves Judgment
of what you did,
And how you did
what you did.
It opens Space
for Self-Forgiveness.

SOUND IS LOOKING FOR ESSENCE

Sound is looking for essence,
    Sound is after your truth,
        Sound is after who you truly are
           without your attitudes.

Sound can teach you
    and divine for you
What your essence is and
    what is what
        you've been calling you.

Regardless of what happened to you
Regardless of your birth experience
    of trauma,
        Regardless of your packaging
Regardless of your position in life.

Sound just wants you
    to stand in your
Position of rightfulness,
    in your starhead,
        in your brilliance.

SOUNDPRINTS EXPLAINED

In-between cell NOTES are threads, acting as bridges . . .
acting as movement,
as responses
SoundPrints are acting as a
    connection
    acting as a respite
In-between notes are the Sounds before I
   translated them into Words.

Please say them
   a lot or a little
Please at least
   look at them
     look at the
       visualness
         of the
           cadence.
As it is most
          helpful for,
    encouraging
       courage and
       openness
       to continue

These are the phonetic
    Spellings of the Sounds

As you see, it takes a lot
    more words to say
       what the sound says
As Sound depersonalizes the stories.

SOUNDPRINT OF OUR BRILLIANCE AND ESSENCE
(Track 4)

She la ti
She la ti
Ka la so fa la ti
Ka la so falati
Me ti la so
me ti la so
Se va ma so
Ma kala
Makala so fa la
Va la so ma
Makala so fa la
Valosomo kala
Jé mé té la So fa la Sé la
Sé la kala So fa So.

BLENDING FORMS

Sound breaks up crystallization
    Sound gets out of the way
        of itself

    Sound humanizes
        Sound includes

    Sound is a universal
        language

    That helps us
        remember and
          shape
            essence

Sound keeps us moving
    When the mind
    Wants to stick
        Somewhere

    These Sounds were first
    These Sounds were before these words

      I translated the sounds
        into words
          and then I translated
           the words
             into sound

    A blending of Forms

SPIRAL EXAMPLES

Spiral is physical
Spiral is psychological
Spiral is origin

Spiral versus Linear thinking
Spiral is a way of unraveling linear
Spiral is efficient
Spiral goes toward accuracy

Spiral is a way of evolving

Spiral is the natural order

Spiral is the planet

Spiral is the Milky Way

Spiral is my finger print
Spiral is my breath print
Spiral is my head print

Spiral is movement
    any time
    any where
    You'll find it fairly certain in

a current in the air.

SPIRAL PHYSICAL

When we look at our bodies
    and touch our bodies
        we find curves, roundness.

There are not any straight lines
    in our bodies
The myth of straightness, linearity
in the physical form is just that,
      a myth.

When we look at our fingerprints
we see our uniqueness
      in the spiral
and that design in a variety of curves
    is realized over this entire body.

Every aperture fits into another aperture
    in spiral direction.

We even see rotation at every joint

We even know that to walk,
asymmetry must be engaged.

This inherent essence
lives within our creative organs
    our re-productive process.

The penis, a cone-shaped, spiral
    form
enters an egg-shaped spiral vortex,
    vagina

The sperm spirals as it travels
    through the Fallopian tubes
      and meets and fertilizes the egg
And, if there is not any interference
the baby spirals, curves and turns
itself
        right out of the
           birth canal.

HUM AS FOOD-ONE'S SOUND SIGNATURE
(Track 2)

Take your speaking voice of today.
How do you say your name if asked?
Just how does your voice sound now?
With the amount of sleep you've had,
what you've eaten,
how you are feeling
where you are, literally.
Say your name and let it
spiral and curve inside your
mouth so it turns and moves
itself into a hum.

This is not a singing note or a right pitch.
It is your tone of the day.
This feeds information to your Body
that you are in Acceptance of
how you are in this moment.
You let your voice match you.

The Nervous System loves to hear and feel your Hum. The hum feeds your Central
Nervous System.
It nourishes
Your voice, is food for your System.
Hum and place your hands at your head.
Move to your heart, your Belly.
Your hum starts massaging your interior landscape.
You move your hands over your body,
feeding and remembering that
you are a three-dimensional body . . .
front, sides and back . . .

TUNING THE BLUES TO GOLD

and your humming is able to touch your
interior dimensions.

Taking your arms and moving them,
circle your Body (Arms extended)
Front, Back, above, Below . . .
using your Hum to create a Boundary for yourself.

Use your Hum to start Creating a Sonic Discernment System.
Use your Hum daily,
to nurture your Central Nervous System
to promote Rest and relaxation.
Use your Hum to Neutralize your Emotional System.
Use your Hum as a Magnet to Draw You to You.

LISTENING TO PREFERENCE

Why is it so important to
    know about the spiral design
of the body for sounding,
      you ask . . .

Because that is what creates
      the accuracy.
That is what allows the Body
    the ability to absorb the
        Sound
    to embody its Sound
    to evolve and involve the Flesh.

The Spiral gives you the cue
    as when you physically
      touch a body
with Sound or hand
    and you meet resistance
The inherent intelligence
    is saying . . . go
        another
           direction.

'Cause going against one's design
    creates dissatisfaction
    Engages the place
      that says
      "I'm not enough."
      "I can't do it right."

And on and over again, the same
                    old melody.
So, the shape and direction
        of the current
                is the plan.
Be willing to go into a
            place of tone
        as soon as you feel
                yourself resonating
        Listen to it and follow
        And don't try to get
                more from
                it than it
                        has to give

and it will always be changing
        as that's how
                it lives.
        And, as you become willing
            to change the
            frequency,
        that's what gives
                you the
        thread, that entwines
                the tune . . .
                you can
                        strum . . .
                        after a while.

SOUNDPRINTS OF OUR PREFERENCE
(Track 4)

Sa Le May

Sa Lo may

Kray ka laso may

Kray kee kray ka la sa mo may

Kray kee kray ka la sa mo may

Kray kee ka la so mo may kray

ka lo sa ma E

Fa ma lo-se

Fa mo lo se

Kay ka lo-se

ma lo se

Supporting the Body
to Move (Release)
the Past Stories
(Memories)

Gives the Body
Room for
the Future

"If you meet resistance - go another direction"
Judith Aston

OUR COMMONALITY

These are stories that have
   lived in the molecular memory
      for thousands of years.

These are body-stories revealed
   to me through my years of
      private practice.

These are sounds that have been
   translated into words.

These are stories the mind has
   made up about what the
      body feels.
These are stories of how life
   has touched most folks.

These are stories that come from
   one session.
These are stories that help
    unravel holding patterns
    in the tissue.

These are familiar stories
These are universal stories.
These are stories that
   do not live truthfully alone.

But together with other stories
that come before or after or under
or over, they make sense of how
the body may have come up
with its own tale.

These stories are one layer . . .
A session
A variety of characters,
A variety of Geometry and colors.

This is A story of A Way to
unravel Denied,
unexpressed sound in our Bodies
So that there will be allowed more
acceptance and permission to
embody OUR Wholeness.

   Spirits Becoming Human Beings.
Human Beings Becoming Loved.

THE WELL-CELL SPIRAL

Now, I'm not trying to sound the root of all that may be denied.
I'm just trying to find
  and listen,
    and respect
the pathway of unraveling the holding patterns.

When I have spoken of linear sounding . . . the "Linear Process"
I am speaking to the belief system that says
  "Let's go to the root of this and take it out."
  "Let's muscle our way through it."
   "Grin and bear it"
    "No pain, no gain."

Also, no Grace
  Mercy,
    Compassion or understanding of
      the intricacies and intelligence
   of this Emotional Memory.

For us truly to be able to heal
  and mature
   and evolve
our emotional bodies,
we need to truly feel safe
  understood and
   appreciated
for our incredible intelligence to have made it this far.

  We need to believe that healing is possible.

There is a cell that lives
  within us
that knows it is well
that knows it is wise

that knows all there is
      to know
      about remembering
         self
            as a whole.
This cell is whole and well
And shines and pulsates its
      glimmering self
to be received
to be believed
to try and get us
      to agree
         to Be.

This cell stands alone . . . it seems
      impossible as it may be
         as the other cells scream
            "you can't be seen
      We have to heal first
         before you beam
            full steam."

Ah, the denial has been great
      to keep the fate of our estate
         in the hands
            of those who are afraid
      that this well cell
         might escape
            our fate.

Could it be possible,
      given our past
         given our credits
            and merits
      that this one cell
         could actually
            Heal the rest of us?

Very Little is Personal . . .

Sound is a tool
for Discernment.

What's mine,
What's not
mine

Initially much
isn't mine

That's why
much that we
feel isn't
Personal.

Sound de-personalizes.

Sound Neutralizes.

Use
Acceptance
Words
as Prayers
and Mantras
as Food
for
Your
System

SOUNDPRINTS ACCEPTANCE

(Track 4)

Ma ah maah maah maah maah maah maaaahhhh

ah ahammmm ah maaaammmm ah . . . . .mmmmmm . . . .mmmmmm-
mm . . . .   -ah . . . . mmmm

eheeeeehhheeeeeeheee

mahhhhhhhhhhhh

MAAHHHHHHHHH

MAHAMahahahahahahahah

eaeaeah-eh-eh-eh-eh-mmmmmmmmm

mmmmmmmmmmmmmmmms

SOUNDING SESSION ACCEPTANCE BLUEPRINT

Sound gets the mind out of the way.
Sound gets the mind out of being the
Authority for the Body.

The stories the mind says:

"You better not voice your anger or
you'll hurt someone or blow up the town!"

"You better not voice your sadness or, girl,
you'll become overwhelmed!"

"You'll lose control!"

"Better not voice your fear or
you'll become paralyzed!"

So, in these sound sessions, what takes place is . . .
the stories the mind has been telling lose power
because . . .
that isn't what takes place.
The body's intelligence does not want us to
"go crazy."
People start being able to hear
in a variety and range of possibilities
How the emotions can be expressed and followed
to a place of tone, integration and acceptance.

Acceptance of what you see
Acceptance of what you be
Gold comes pouring in and through
All the space that is you.
Acceptance is the Healer,
Acceptance is the Window
Acceptance is the space and place
of Grace.
Grace is not in judgment
or Punishment or Reward
of Past, Present or Future Stance.

PRAYER PRINT FOR DISCERNMENT
(Track 5)

CShee CShee Cshee Schee
Show me Ku á ti
Ku á ti
Sé ma sé me
Shree Schree Schree
La Sa Vala Sa Vala
Shree ati Shree áti
So Che la So
So khe la So
Ma ka la So
Ma So Ve la to
Ma So Vo la la to
Ka á lo sé
ma kala toe
Toe mé ke lo so vala to Ka Va le to
Ka Va lo té lo so va lo kala
So Va lo ke la

SOUNDING SESSION FOR DISCERNMENT

Sounding what is not ours . . .

So much chatter, static,
    folds upon folds
        layer upon layer,
    of not being heard,
      or feeling regret
      for what was said
            or done.

Mis-understandings,
    mis-interpretations
      all through the system.

Most times, at this layer of
          unraveling,
    the sounds or prose
    are not very personal.
It is just a product of
    the various degrees and
      angles of the geometry
    of the History of a
        holding pattern.

That's why it is called
      Sounding that which is
      not ours:
It's what we have taken on
It's what happens with any wound
    that has not healed.
The wound becomes an opening, a magnet
    for thoughts, feelings that get
    into the range of its drawing power.

SOUND SESSIONS

A Sounding session of what
    is not ours
is sounding that which
      has already become conscious,
        that is no longer in
          denial,
      that has already been
          processed.

It is not a re-telling
    or a re-living of our story.
It is a story taken
    and evolved to present
      time
    maturing the emotional body.

A Sounding Session is Sounding
      the denial system
Sounding the unexpressed anger
    suppression, sadness, depression,
    joy, love, lust, racism, sexism,
      on and on
Sounding the various judgments.

Sounding our various desires and
    needs to be loved, heard,
      felt, acknowledged

Sounding the sounds of these
    denied feelings being denied.
Sounding these sounds to awaken our rhythms.

SPIRAL DISCERNMENT
(Track 5)

REMEMBERING

*Just making Room,
Getting Current
with Past, Present
and Future
Memories*

REMEMBERING

Amnesia seems to be a
great obstacle to sustaining
consciousness.
The opportunity of acquiring amnesia
is infinite.

I suppose that one of the
prevailing systems that
creates this epidemic
is the denial system
That seems to be taught in
almost all of our institutional forms,
such as in our educational
systems, in our governments,
And in many religious organizations.

Closed Systems
Support
Amnesia,
Paralysis,
inability to
Remember
that we are here
to Connect with our
Greatness
not our Fear.

REMEMBERING (1)

Remembering is a question
    of concern
        for us
            who wonder
                and wish
                    and desire
                        to know

what we knew
    before we could
        say aloud
            and be heard
            of our
                knowings
                    of such things
                        as wisdom

Remembering is a time you know so well
    that you remember
        how to move
            and turn
                and yearn
      to let the sun
            shine in
                on the
                many
            arrays and covers of
    tapestries that veiled
            what you know that
    You remember what you knew
                before Now.

REMEMBERING (2)

Everyone that I have
    ever worked with
        Remembers a time
          when they
              remembered
                  more than they
                      know now.

And this memory
    is what causes the pain,
        Pain causes the anguish,
        Anguish causes the shame,
        Shame of not remembering.

And, these feelings
    are what rev
        the motor
    Fire the Soul
        move the System
            to say
                please
                    please
    Let me release my sleep.

REMEMBERING (3)

How do we Remember
   How do we regain
      the trust
   How do we take
      the risk
   How do we let
   ourselves
    be in
     Not-Remembering?

We use our sound
   of hurt
We use our sound
   of grieving
  our loss
   of memory
We use our sound
   to break up crystallization
    of Amnesia

We use our sound
   to feed the brain
   to massage
    this muscle
   to awaken
    again.

REMEMBERING (4)

You let the Sounds
   dislodge the debris
    the encrustation
    from time
      not spent
    dwelling in knowing.

SOUNDPRINT ESSENTIALS
REST, TRUST, QUIET
(Track 6)

Sé Valamé khé alo

Sé Valamé khi alo

Se Volomé khialo

Sha sa sa mo . . .

Sha Sa . . .

mo . . .

Sha sa . . .

mo . . .

Khe la soma

Khe la so ma . . .

Khe la so ma . . .

Chi yo la ah

Chi yola ah . . .

So mé chi lo

Sa va lo

A Daily Practice

We begin with
Emotional Expression
(whining, moaning, bitching)

to get Quiet Enough
(Humming into silent Hum)

to Be able to Listen
and trust our Resting

to Let Go
and Breathe and
Nourish
our Central Nervous
System.

It's an
Everyday
Affair
to Create a
Vortex of
Transformation

"If you accept the process it turns into light
Acceptance + Humor + Gold"
Elias DeMohan

SELF-PRAYER IS ESSENTIAL WORK

Talking to
Self

Talking and Praying
to one's
Essence

to one's
Wellness
to come forth and
Have Courage
to Live
Essence
is
An Essential
Prayer

THE BLUES

There's No Separation
from Past
Blues
and Current
Blues
and/or
Future
Blues

TRANSFORMING THE BLUES INTO GOLD

Transforming the Blues into Gold is taking
    the meaning that is not
        connected and bringing
            it into consciousness.
Taking that grief that hasn't been
    expressed or felt fully enough
    in the body and
        embodying it.

Doesn't seem to work moving
    feeling with the mind.
    When the story gets to
        be told through the body
            with sound . . . there
        is a vibration, a
            pulsation, an
                internal movement.

What is frozen, gets vibrated, agitated
    A frequency gets ignited,
            there's fire,
The will gets fired, engaged
    Sound is an internal
            experience,
    an inside job.

We haven't gotten to the Root
    of the Blues, we're just
        talking content:

"This happened to me
    and this happened to me
        and this happened to me."

THE BLUES

They are all still hurt
   They are all still angry
      They are all still sad
      They are all feeling rejected

        and this happened to me.

        Emotion has sound and is
           tied into the rhythm;
        emotions are a highly
           intelligent and a highly
             refined system.

The Blues are being allowed a big
      piece of this system
      as it has been denied
        for so long.

    We all feel it so deeply.
    Not listening to
      Our Soul
          That is the Big Blues.

The Blues of not feeling whole
    and knowing that we are
      and could be.
The Memory that is being denied
  is our wholeness
        and that's the Blues.

THE WAILING WALL'S PURPOSE

I sing my Blues
   to ignite the root of
      my sadness
I sing my Blues
   to ignite my fire
I sing my Blues
   to engage my
      will
I sing my Blues to the
   many vessels
      of my body
I sing my Blues
   to a place of hope
I sing my Blues
   to a place of
      remembering
   when I didn't feel
      Blue
I sing my Blues
   to honor them
I sing my Blues
   to honor myself

Sing your Blues
  Sing your Sorrows
     Sing your pain into their songs
And they shall be released
    moved transformed

Tears of this century prepared
the ground for a new spring
for the future

YOU GOT THE BLUES?

This book is about the Blues,
The many varieties and hues
                    of blue,
The many aspects attributed
            to the Malady
                        of the Blues,

You got the Blues?
            I got the time.
You got the Blues?
            I'll find a rhyme.
You got the Blues
            I'll give you it's
                        Prime
                        time
                        of listening
                        of ingesting
                        of filtering
                        of living
            My pallet
                        with only
                        the finest
            Hue of the
                        BLUE

Cause I'm looking for the precision
            not just the given
                        of the story.

THE BLUES

I want the source to embark upon
    the very
        essence
        of the art
    of singing the Blues.
Don't just give me
        I only can
            if you will
        and you probably
            won't
        so I won't
            first
And then you
            can feel
        the rejection
            of love
        at it's source
            over and over again
But you'll think it's me
    so I win.

Trigger Points

"Not Good Enough"

"Still Not Enough"

Self Doubt
creates
Confusion
creates
Denial

BLUES CREPT IN AGAIN

Blues crept in again
Been hovering around
      just to get in
   and cringe my gut
and tear at my womb
     and bring me
         nothing
But this God-forsaken
         gloom.

The Blues again
we sure are kin
never too far away
from each other's skin

And, I bend to let them in
and I cry for them to end
     But I'm bone dry at
         my skin
so I break and get thin
to their ready blend
         of me.

They shook me through and through
they're nothing except the Blues
They don't care how they're used
     just for the taking
     just for the breaking
   for the hue of my Blues
     they'll do
     me and you
        too
Blues don't lose . . . they fuse
     with you.

The blues are lots of class
lots of soul
the blues are life and they are everywhere.

The blues are blood, blue blood
The rhythm and beat of the body is the blues.

The biggest blues is not feeling connected
       to Mother-Father-God.

You got a list of blues as big as the sky.
Blues are anything you want to talk about,
Blues are the womb

Blues is victim
It is the spiral
It is tight
It is the holding pattern.

You said . . .

I said . . .

What?

SPIRAL MIS-COMMUNICATION
(Track 6)

HO HO HO HO HO HO HO HO HO HO HO HO HO HO HO HO HOWL HOWL HOWL HOWL HOWO HOWO HOWO OHOW OHOW OW OW OWL OWL OWL OWL owl owl ohown en ouwn en en en en sense any make doesn't it on should have said no I hadn't said That's not what I meant wish that

000 000 000 000 OMMMMmmm

We Can't deny the
Blues
Blues are at the
Insertion
of Mis-Communication.

Appreciation For the Language of the Body

Our Form
has it's own language.

Slow,
rhythmic
Pulse
Here
How to Feel
and Listen
Big-Wide
Spatial design

I want to
Listen
Myself
Back
into Rhythm

HOPE IS TRANSFORMING

Sounding the Blues is being
    willing to match the
        frequency, the particular
            rhythm, the direction
or blueprint of the Anger,
    frustration, the depression,
and all the variety of emotional
    components of its
        pathway and
            then following it.
    A dialogue is begun
      A relationship is beginning.

It might begin as a grunt,
A moan, a child crying
    and guiding you and
        bending you into
    a beautiful open-mouthed
      vowel or
        Harmonics.

And you don't have to
    know where your
      blues are leading
        you,
    but you can always know that
    if you follow, your
        blues will come into
      a tone of acceptance
        and integration

and hope will start
              being built.
    There's no separation from
        past blues and current
              Blues.

The words/sounds are memories
    of the same age,
Similar rhythm and emotional
    component, whether it
      happened yesterday
        or thirty years ago.

It's geometry we are talking
    about here.
    If it's past Blues. . . more
        intensity.
If you got all those past
    Blues all you gotta do
    is get one more
         Blue.

All you need is one more
    person to step on your
toe (accidentally). You might have yelled at first
    and after a while you just
      might shoot
'Cause the Blues got
    piled up so much.

HUM AS MAGNET EXERCISE
(Track 6)

Speak your name over and over,
let it spiral and spin into a hum.
Give expression to your sadness, to your blues,
use the vowels of big open-mouthed AH's and big wide, round O's;
stay in it until you find your attention starts wandering,
that's your cue to start winding wherever you are with your sound
back to your hum.
After awhile your hum becomes a magnet.
It helps bring you back to yourself.
That is why the hum is the foundation for your
Emotional Anatomy.
It keeps you safe when you go out there to express your unexpressed.
It is the thread to bring you home.

BLUEPRINT OF HOPE

Hope lives in the geometry;
    Hope lives in the experience
        of the Blues moving into
            a place of bigger dimension
        by following its inherent
        Blueprint.

Hope lives in the experience of
    listening and accepting what's
        there as the blueprint
            that the acceptance
    of the feeling is what
            allows the movement
    that allows the possibility of maturing
        the emotional
            body.

Hope lives in the geometry
    of the maturing blueprint.
Hopefulness is when people
    can voice themselves without going
        crazy, without going nuts,
            or losing it,
    or going over the edge,
            or getting overwhelmed,
            or getting beaten up.

Hope is the knowing that the
    emotions are a highly intelligent
        system and do not want to
    be left in the past . . . but want
    to join the evolution.

Hope is in
Knowing
There is Intelligence
in the
Blueprint

SOUNDPRINT OF TRANSFORMING THE BLUES IMPRINT
(Track 7)

kri ka la ka kri
kri da la ka Icri
kri ka la ka kri
Shiva sa la ki
She mo a se
She mo a se
She mo a se
Shi vi al a ti
Ne mi ati
ni mi ati

Kwal ati
Kwal ati
Me u to
Me u to

PHYSICAL BODY RHYTHM AND BLUES

*Beginning
of
the
common tales,
the
Emotional Anatomy Conditioning
our
stories
are made of*

Disassociation
is Having its
Day
We can't get
our Healing
if We're not
Here.

BEGINNING OF RELEASE OF
SLEEP

You better get on your feet
    and weep
   if you need to
But be prepared to keep
    your meet
   with your Destiny
   Be prepared to meet
        your gap
   your lack
    your slack
     of will
If you want to release your sleep
   you can't keep
your deep desire to
creep
   as if you could
go this way without me

I'm with you all the way

EXERCISE FOR TOUCHING FEAR
(Track 7)

Sometimes the fear feels so big
that it paralyzes us.
It tells us that there is no way to express it
or move it.
It can even tell us that it is all there is.
We find a place in our body, maybe the upper heart area
and we pat ourselves gently there
and let ourselves softly say our sounds or words in a whisper.
Let the sounds be small,
let them honor the size of the opening.
The fear may be huge
but usually the opening to release is very small.
Let the whispered sounds move into a hum.
We are wanting to establish trust.
Gently sounding and humming to ourselves
starts melting the paralyzed, frozen fluid.
Remember we are 70% fluid
REGARDLESS.

Emotional Expression
needs Body
Movement
Please Listen
to Your
Body
and Breathe

BEGINNING TO AWAKEN HONESTY

I speak honestly,
    But I don't tell all
I speak freely
    But I don't say when
I speak boldly,
    But I don't always bend
  to All
    Not All
       Not All

I do not bend
  I do not let the wind
    move me
      until
    I can no longer
      twill
        your rhythm

SOUNDPRINTS OF AWAKENING WANT-A-BE

es en a la ho
   esen
      es sen ne a la ho a lei
      es senne alaha a leie

e s sende a le he a mo sen na lep o
   es si a la ho se ah
     sim me ala
     sim me alo
es sin ne a maho

          a swa te ta
         eh la boho se la ta
       ke la ha i a liati
       asine a be a la enti
    sien me a lo so
    min a lo ho so
          bien la
    a sin a la ha la ch
    alahole
      alahalale
   alaholole
   alaholale
   alaholale
   alaholale
    alaholale
    alaholale
    alaholale

A la ah lo ko te em em alo
  ala mo bo mo bo mo bo po
  alo mo ba bo asa a la
  ma ma ma ma bo ti
    ma se alaen

A RESTING FORMULA

We begin with
Emotional Expression
(release)

to get quiet enough
(pause)

to Be able to Listen
and
Trust our Resting

to be able to
Nourish and Effect
our Central Nervous System

SPIRAL
COMPASSION
(Track 7)

Use
Acceptance
Words
as Prayers
and Mantras
as Food for Your System

COME   PASSION
   COME   PASSION
      COME   PASSION
         COME   PASSION
            COME   PASSION
               COME   PASSION
                  COME   PASSION
                     COME   PASSION
                        COME   PASSION
                     COMPASSION

Racism
Lives
in All
Packages

RACISM SITS HEAVY

Racism sits heavy

    Sits heavy in my heart
    Sits heavy in my soul
        racism sits heavy in my gut

That makes us all afraid
    to say
        "please, doesn't this
            ever stop,
                    end
                    bend
            Somewhere
                in some
                    humanity
                    somewhere?

I'm afraid of you and
    you are afraid of me?"
        We're afraid of our
            shadows
        everywhere we look
It's crooked
    It's mis-took
    Someway, somewhere
        Always.

RACISM

LOOKS LIKE

OTHER-HATRED

BUT LIVES

AS

SELF-HATRED

THE PHYSICALITY OF RACISM AND SELF-HATRED

Sticky,
Mucilaginous
Substance
that I have
found in Bodies . . .

holds
Emotional
Content
that has
become
dense or
opaque

STORED JUDGMENT

Words are not just stored
in our Heads
But . . .
in our tissue, Blood,
organs, cells,
Bone.

YOU SAY

You say, I got the Blues
You say, I feel real bad.
You say, it don't look like
      it's going to get loose.
You say, how to do
You say, what to do
      and when to bend
You say, it can't get no worse
You say, you don't care how
      as long as it don't.

You say, please, please, please
      have some mercy on me.
You say, please, please, please
      let me get free from this freeze
      just some release you say,
          please.

You say, you don't know how you went wrong
You say, you don't know what is the song
You say, you can't find where you've gone.

You say, please have some mercy
You say, please just some slack
You say, please I need a cushion
You say, please get back.

GOT ANY COLOR GIRL BLUES

I got the White Girl Blues
and I can't shake them loose.
I got the Black Girl Blues
and I can't get a move.
I got the Yellow, Tan, Red and Brown Girl Blues
and nothing turns these blues around.

I've tried many a way
I've tried for many a day
to lose these "you got the any color" Girl Blues.
I've shook
I've hollered and wollared
I've moaned and groaned.

Didn't do me no good
I didn't feel me no better
I didn't feel no worse
I just got the feeling
that I can't be loose.

It's deep in my roots
It's crowding my pores
It's clogged up my lines
It's been around for a very long time
These "any color" Girl Blues.

Do you know how very strange it seems
To not be able to share your dreams
To not be able to look in the mirror
and know that what you're seeing
        is only a glimmer of what is real?

This is the "any color" Girl Blues
This is the disguise
To not be able to mimic

What's before your eyes.
To not be able to voice
that which you know
To not be able to be viewed
from the truth of the roots
       that is Mother.

It's these White Girl Blues
       that is Mother
It's these Black Girl Blues
       that is Mother
It's these Red Girl Blues
       that is Mother
It's these Yellow Girl Blues
       that is Mother
It's these Brown Girl Blues
       that is Mother
Her not being seen any more than me.

The "got the any color" girl blues
Is turning me through and through
It's turning me inside out
It's turning me right side up
It's making me feel
       most of the time
That I'm just fucked up.

It's the "any color" Girl Blues
That's got my attention
It's the "any color" Girl Blues
That I can't even mention
It's the "any color" Girl Blues
That you don't even know
It's the "any color" Girl Blues
That's all I know.

DIAGNOSIS
POWER OF WORDS . . .

These are
      words that
           tighten our
               vessels,
                    compress
                    our circulation,
              reduce love
                 to our
                   HEART

Once you Start
Awakening
that which
is
denied
it is Hard to
deny
that which
is
denied

WATCH

Watch your Words
    Watch your Actions
      Watch your Thoughts
        Watch your Consciousness
        Watch your Heart

If you think you are
    your package . . .
      you'll get lost . . .

I'M NOT WHAT I AIN'T

I'm not white . . . I say
    you say . . . "What?"

I say , I'm not white
    you say . . . "Right!"

I say, I'm not white
you say . . . "YEAH?"

Then what you call
    that white butt of yours?
You say,
What you call
    that white leg of yours?
You say,
What you call
    that white pussy of yours?

I'm not white, I say

    If your not white, baby . . .
    then I better get-back-quick.

I better blow my brains right now.

I better forget everything I ever
                  knew

I better start all over
I better just quit

I better be real quick
If you ain't white

You better get back,
        and you better get quick . . .

'Cause I got a feeling
        I'm not the only
        white witch around here,
        who's slick

I got a feeling we're infiltrating
the white world
        In bigger numbers than we ever
        figured . . .
and you won't know
        'cause it doesn't show.

Oh, come on, you just don't
        wanna be white . . .
        That's what you're saying.

You're just feeling guilty about
        that white skin and
        where all it's been.

You're just feelin' left back,
        'cause you're not black.

You're just feeling . . .

I'm just feeling lost
        I'm just feeling alone
        I'm just feeling nowhere.

I'm just feeling no kin to this skin.
It's Dark inside here
    It's black inside here
    There's no light I can find

I've been giving that light
    ALL away,
Making myself believe that I
    wasn't gray.

Making you believe that I was
    Light.
Making me believe that I didn't
    need to fight.

It's scared inside here
    It's terrified inside here.
It doesn't know what way to go
Let alone know
    what I've been calling flow.

No wonder you think
    I'm white . . .
I've been putting out
    all that light

Making us all agree
    that it was alright
Making it all seem,
    that we'd come out of
    this dream
and just beam ourselves

bright and clean.
I said, I ain't white . . .
    Are you starting to understand?
I said, I ain't white
    that's not about you getting mad!
I said, I ain't white
    It's not a complaint
I said, I ain't white
    Just saying what I ain't.

What are you saying woman?
    Just what you trying to say?
Are you trying to say
    That you ain't what you
        think
        I am
Are you trying to say
    that you ain't what I am
        and you ain't
        what I ain't?

I'm trying to say . . .
    that you're whatever you think
    and that has nothing to do
    with what I ain't.

And, the sooner you get . . . you
    ain't what you think
The sooner I get to get real
    with what I ain't.

As long as you think . . . all is
    what it ain't
The more I walk around feeling

what ain't.
I just want to get straight
    with all what ain't.
And get on with this piece
    of story book hate.

If you think you're white
    then tell me this,

How come your life
    is in such a fix?

And . . . how come all these
    governments
got their foot on your head
And how come each pay day
    You ain't got any bread . . .

And, how come everything's
    getting higher and higher?
And, how come you think if
    you get whiter and whiter
    if you just keep trying a little
                    harder
    be a little more tighter,
You'll be what you ain't
    And . . . you ain't white
I don't care what you think.

You can't get white enough for this crew
    you can't get white enough
                for this world
You can't get white enough
    to make it different
                for you and yours

I ain't white enough . . .
  I ain't black enough . . .
    I ain't red enough . . .
      I ain't brown enough . . .
        and I ain't yellow enough . . .

to join these forces.
And I'm stating it the
only way that I know . . .
        The only route I can take
      The only soul I own . . .
  ain't white
    ain't black
      ain't brown
        ain't red
          and it ain't yellow.

AND . . . I won't let you make
  me think what I ain't,
make me talk what I cain't,
make me pretend what I ain't.
And I ain't what you think.

So what are you if you ain't a color
So what are you if you ain't a package
So what are you if you can't get a little
    cultural conditioning behind
      your behind?

So what are you without your skin
What are you without your pride
Without your rhyme
    of time unending, of your skin
    and it's variety of blending?

TOUGH LOVE . . .

Sometimes is needed
to get the attention
of Deep-ingrained
Paralysis

EXERCISE EEE   EEEE O AH W/ PULSE
(Track 8)

Take the vowels
E E E E
O O O O
AH
E E E E
O O O O
AH

Repeat these vowels several times with a fast, quick pulse
It doesn't matter if the vowels start changing on you, follow them, keep a quick
pulse rhythm
then spiral back to your HUM.
This form of using sound helps to keep the words from getting stuck in you and also
helps to dissolve any judgments that may come up while you read.
Sound helps engage the inherent intelligence of openness.

SOUNDPRINT OF JUDGMENTS
(Track 8)

Ish Vo to lich
        ka la to ma
Ish yo to lash
            ka lo
ish ve alo
        ko ma ta
            ko la ta
                Ka Kal La
                    Lo me
                        ti la
        Ke se la
so ta
        me yo ta
        me yalolfo
        meyalotaljebl

The massage
is to just
keep moving
not to get
into processing
where you
are everytime
you get stuck.
Stuck only means
you need movement
not analysis.

HOPE IS A MOLECULE

Hope is a molecule
Hope is a possibility of a future
    living without suffering

Hope is what you get
when you get ready to let yourself
    follow your bliss . . . nowhere

Hope is hardly nowhere
if you look at what is most of the time
    in your sight

Hope is Gold
Hope is when
    you trust your intelligence

Hope is when you put
your weight into
    your inner knowing

Hope is when you
take the risk to
    follow your Blues

Blues Breath Exercises
(Track 8)

The diaphragm area is sometimes considered the Emotional Brain Center

Place your hands firmly at your solar plexus/diaphragm area

so that you can feel the expansion and contraction
of your breathing and the movement of your ribcage.

Breathe open-mouthed
so that you can hear your breath
slowly inhale and exhale
feeling the expansion and contraction

laugh from the the diaphragm
dramatic
AH-HA-HA

Inhale - release an audible strong HA
HA
HA
HA
HA
HA
that is plenty.

It doesn't take much sound;

come back to your open mouth breathing.

This sound and breath are very helpful for breaking up crystallization,
paralysis
warms us up
helps us notice how we feel
helps get weight into the lower body.

GOING DEEPER INTO BLUES

The blues run deep
The blues don't sleep
The blues can't keep
you from knowing
your blues.

Your history follows you
like it's tracking a star
it knows when to step in
and grab a few bars
of your peace
of your calm
of your moment of
tranquillity.

All you need to do
is just get a little tight
feel a bit of fright
and the blues
takes a bite
and doesn't let go
until you show
all you know.

PLEASE USE THE BLUES TO IGNITE YOUR WILL

The pain is necessary to feel.
               Do not attempt to not feel
The pain and the fear and the terror of it all,
It is being healed by being experienced.

Our Blues are a form of
               connecting to our roots.
Use our Blues,
Use the blues to connect,
               to ignite our feeling.

Taking the Blues
               into Gold
        is an experience
of healing the emotions.

We cannot keep
               the blues "blue"
               the blues are "gold."

REST IS WHAT I NEED TO FEEL
STRESS IS WHAT I GET

So you ever get so tired of the
stress of not having the rest
of what you need
to really be
free
from your debts?

This is the test, boys and girls
that has us going, boys and girls
to keep us real distracted
to the point of abstraction
to what our true
purpose
attraction 'is'

It keeps us worried
It keeps us angry
It keeps us tired
It keeps us drinking
It keeps us bothered
It keeps us embodied
by our fears
of being a percentage
of the unemployed
the homeless
the forgotten
the betrayed

It works . . . it works real good
'cause we get so distracted
we don't remember . . . or we
remember . . . but it's so painful
'cause we're not working,
but it is

It's enough to make you want
to give up
to spit up
All your worth
and cry "help . . . I can't do it anyhow
anymore"

anyway
I'm tired of not having
the rest
of what I need
to rest
into what I need
to rest

Rest is what I need to feel
Rest is what I need to feel
Rest is what I need to feel
is rest

One myth of Apollo
was that the people
would bring their
grievances and suffering
to him and he would
sing their blues and
they would lose
them.

IF YOU WOULD SING YOUR BLUES

If you would sing your Blues
If you would move your Blues

If you would sing your Blues
you would move your Blues

If you would sing your Blues
you would move your Blues

To lose your blues
you've got to loose your blues
you've got to move your blues
to groove your blues
to croon your blues
you've got to let yourself
be blue
with a little red
with a little head
you've got to nudge those
blues
you've got to give it red
you've got to give it head
you've got to meet it
dead
in front of you
Those blues can't be fooled by
any half-willed let-me-go
melody
They got to be true

to their hue
and to your belly
Those blues
only move . . . when you groove

to your blues
to your blues
you move
to your blues
you carry
to your blues
you nary . . .
linger

Without knowing
you've been
blue
you are blue
you are
your blues

So sing your blues if you
want to lose them
Sing your blues if you want
to loose them
Sing your blues if you
want to live your life
you sing your blues
to the sky
you sing your blues
to the sky
you sing your blues
to the sky.

SING THE BLUES TO REST FORMULA

This is to allow rest
within rest comes movement
within movement comes trust
within trust comes compassion
within compassion comes cooperation
within cooperation comes transformation

I honor that I am a seed
nurturing my gentle
loving qualities

SING THE BLUES TO REST SOUND PRINTS
(Track 8)

A se la tio
    uh ha i e luo
      m m m m m m m m m m
         m m m m m m m m m m m
           m m m m m m m m m m m m
             m m m m m m m m m m m m m
             Harmonics

eh la eh lo ah se o la
    Ah eh ohhhhhhhhhh
      Ah eh ohhhhhhhhhhh
        Ah eh ohhhhhhhhhhh
          Ka ma la so ma oh me

eh la mo ma ma
    Ah se eh a O
      e si a mo
        na se oh mo ma ma

eh o mo ma - eh O
    O - O - O
      eh - eh - eh

Se me a me la se
    a me la se a
      me la se
        a sne la se
          ea me
            go ta me

SPIRAL OF BLUES TO REST
(Track 8)

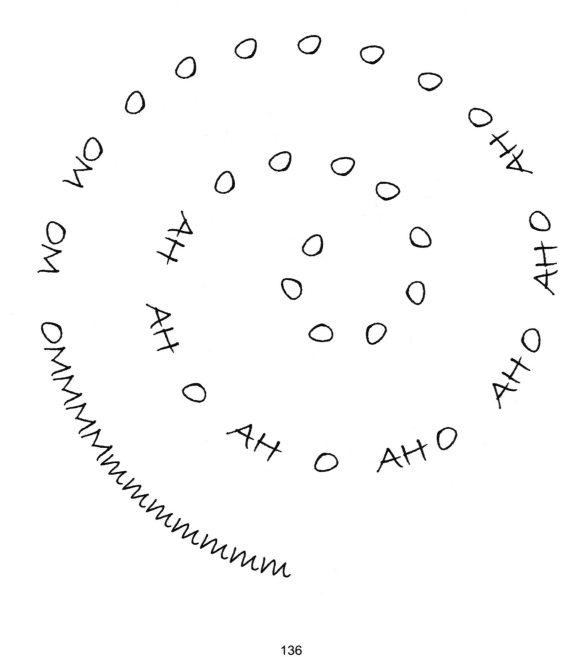

Please be
Encouraging to the
Emotional/Feeling
Body.

You're doing Great,
So Brave,
So Courageous
Go on . . .

Now we're going Deeper

GRIEF I

I'm mad you're dead
    It's bad you're dead
    Damn it, I'm like lead
    Since you're dead

Where are you?
    What's it like?
How goes, you?
    Is it all right?

Do you remember where you've been?

Do you know what you've seen?
    Do you exist as you were?
    Are you molecules of stars?
    Are you energy pores of life?
Are you regenerating and regrouping
    for another time?

Who are you now?
    Do we still talk?
    Do you still care?
Or is it just dark and gone
    away from here?

Like how I feel so many days
    that you're dead
    and I'm not really alive
either.

GRIEF II

It's a lie that you're dead
    You're alive in my head.

You're in my life.
    Am I in yours?

Do I still influence you?
    As you do me?

Did I go with you
    As you stayed with me?

Do I just not know
    How to be without you?

Why is this so hard?

I feel you trying to talk to me
I have you in my dreams

I don't know what you mean to say
I don't know what it seems

I only know there are no seams
and nothing seems to be as it seems.

GRIEF III

Another death
    Another form gone
    Another month or year of grieving

Another days and weeks of anger
    And irritation
    and not feeling good . . .
'Cause another died
    Another touched me and died
    Another moved me and died
And I keep dying, I keep living
    And I keep trying to figure out why.

And, I know the day will come
    When I don't ask why.
And, I know the day will come
    When I will be all right.
And, then another phone will ring
    And, it will be another
      Day and I will hear
Another died
    Another form gone
      Good-bye.

SOUNDPRINT GRIEF REMEMBERS
(Track 8)

Awh Ahw o-o-oh-oh-oh-
awh awwh awwh
o o h oh oh
Sé ahwh sé ahwl
ol llh ol ol

Mégaahso Mégaahso
Mé gaahso méga

Pisame gohalso
pisame gohalso

So magalaohosola

Oh ohohlohloho

TIMING CONCEPT

The blueprint of this emotional
geometry
follows a spiral,
It is not a neat formula
it is not a straight line
that you start here
and go there.
It is an unwinding, it is like
opening a safe,
it is how the roots
grow
a little this way,
a little over here,
it is a design for listening.

Listening: if a person can
really be listened to,
they can stop telling their
story.
It's the same principle with the
memory feelings
within the tissue.
If the memories-of-feelings
get to sing their songs
they get to move . . .
possibly to other songs.

The timing of the geometry
of the memories-of-feelings
is usually . . . a faster rhythm
than the tissue rhythm.
So, we truly must practice
Listening . . .
    to the intelligence of the tissue
  If we stay too long
      Linger too much
        in the story
          or content
          of the sound
      this becomes indulgence
    this is more the timing
      of the mind
        determining the
          movement of
            the feelings in
              the body.

Our job is to turn
  over this work
    to the inherent
      intelligence of
        the body.

Remembering that it
  Would never serve
    the intelligence to
      go beyond what
        it has support
          for . . .
    This is the pattern we are wanting to
        interrupt
    This I am calling
      indulgence.

LISTENING IS . . .

Listening seems to be the most
important ingredient.

In my listening
I'm listening to hear my story.

When my story
gets it's listening

I hear my healing.

I want to listen myself
            back
                    into
                            rhythm.

Listening is compassion and acceptance
of all we have been, said and done.

SOUND TOUCHES PLACES THAT
HANDS CANNOT REACH

There is no longer any need
to rehash our stories or content.
The goal is to surrender
the place of judgment.

BOUNDARIES ARE THE BEGINNING OF REST

Boundaries are not a fixed position
Without them we can keep ourselves from
     being able to stay in commitment
     to the next step,
          next layer.

Boundaries let us move
     toward our framework
     and feel our dimensions,
          the space we occupy
the same way we swaddle a baby
     that the baby can feel something
          to push against
     So it knows where
          it begins
          and where something
          else starts.

Boundaries are the Beginning
     of having Rest
We can rest into ourselves
     when we know
     where we are
          literally.

SPIRAL DISHARMONY INTO TRUE TONE OF BLUE
(Track 9)

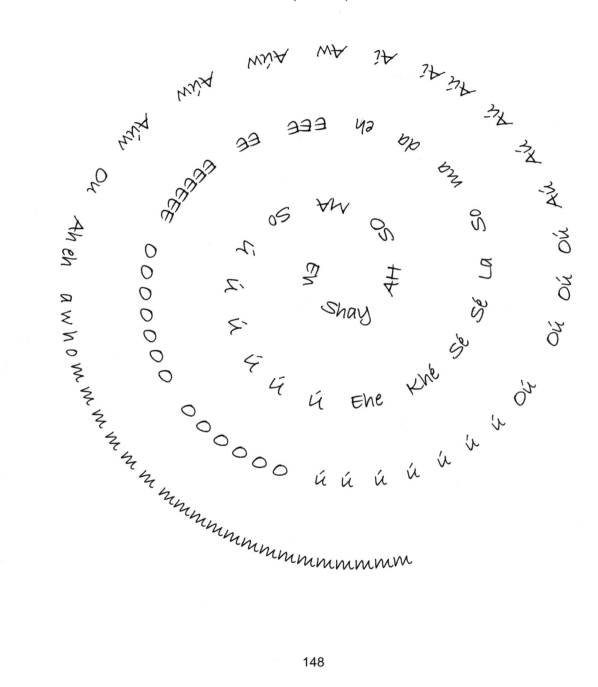

RAGE AND TERROR RUN THE SHOW

Fear,
Terror,
Anger,
Rage,

Seem to be the
underlying imprint
that is prevalent and
familiar to most
systems, packages,
Lineages, Groups, and
Individuals.

We may need to
Expand our memory of
Imprints.

Fear and Anger are not enough
Reason to not do our Work.

I MUST find another source for CONNECTION
than to my fear and paralysis

SOUNDPRINT OF RHYTHM OF ANGER
(Track 9)

Se Ka ye
  Se Ka Se Ka
  Se Ka
       Lo ti
  Ka Kha
       Khi
  Se Ke
       La
       Ka
       Sa
            Ka
            La Sa
  Me Ke SA
  Ka Le Ghi me te

       TA KA . . . TA KA . . .
  Ta-Ka . . . Ta-KA

  Tohka te sa ma ka la to ama toka

  eh ka le to te ka

            se ka lo te me

  ka to ka ta ka ta ka ta ka ta
  TA KA . . . TAKA TAKAHHHH TAH

ANGER ISN'T ALL THAT WORDY

Anger has a bad reputation . . .
    A lot of opinions
      it evokes.
A most difficult expression
      to Emote
    without hurting Someone
     with the power
       of our Words
         and the feelings
           Behind them.

The Sound Behind Anger
    is a Powerful Source
      of Revenue
        Being Spent
          like a Large
           Fragment.

Words can kill, People say . . .
    Seems like Words stay
    in the Body for as
      Long as ever.

The words of Anger embedded
    in the Body are
      Great
    we know Verbal
      Abuse many
        Times takes
        Longer to heal the body
from the words
       that went in
         than the imprint
         of physical touch.

Although, we shan't
  Compare Abuse
or of what suffers us the most.
  Just to Emphasize
   The Power of Words . . .
  as in any
    Diagnosis . . .
We must cease fighting
  everyone and everything

Residue of Hate
Molecules

Hating that which
hates us
kills us
One way or
Another

UNRAVELING THE HATE

HATE keeps us Bound
    To the unending cycle
      of Re-Birth
        and Despair.

HATE keeps us at the
    Mercy of
      Those we HATE

HATE Wants us to HATE
    It's how it gets
      It's Juice,
        It's way
          with US.

All the Words and Acts
    of Ghandi
All the Words and Acts
    of King
Were trying to help us
    Unbind
    from the Cruel
      FATE
        of
        HATE.

That's why They Laugh
    At us when
      We hate them,

Jeer and Tease
    us to HATE
      them yet more.

Keep us off
    our Track
    Keep us Hating
That's the game
    That's the "Stuck-on-Stupid."

Don't Let them
    Keep us
      Hating.
The People we
    HATE
    Control us
Control our
    FATE.

THE PHYSICALITY OF HATE AND FEAR

Molecules
Congeal
Protoplasm

Become
Crystallized

HATE & FEAR
Creates
Crystallization
in any System

circulatory system
lymphatic system
central nervous system
glandular system . . .

Guilt is a Big one
    that you must grace
in all honesty with yourself
    and a sound can help.
        Sound can make you honest.

SPIRAL OF WHINE HATE AND FEAR
(Track 10)

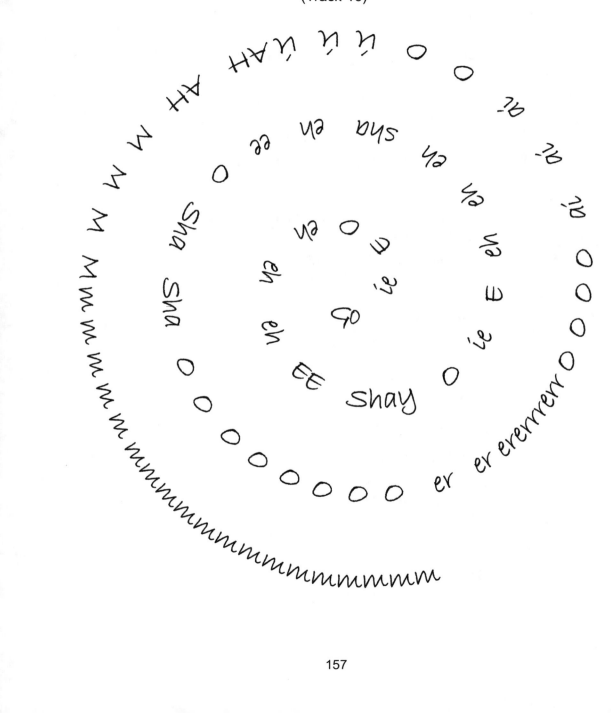

GUILT IMPRINT (INVERTED PRIDE)

I'm asking and suggesting
    in many forms
that you do not hang-out too long
      in what's wrong.
Give it its time-slot
    but only as long
          as it feels true to your innards
          not to your guilt potential.

How do you know
    When it's guilt that is running the show?
Guilt has no end
    Guilt has no beginning
          Guilt is there wanting more guilt
            and support.
Guilt tells you
You're not good enough
      to rest.
You're not loved enough
      to get.
    What your healing is calling for.

Guilt tells you the story
      of ages past
    That so and so
      isn't good enough
        and cannot last.

Guilt is another word
    for racism, sexism,
        separatism of the classes.

Guilt can set in
by saying Yes when we mean No.

Guilt sets in
by not listening to our Instinct from God.
Guilt turns into self doubt.

Self Doubt turns
into self-deprecating thinking and action.

Amnesia sets in
and we feel abandoned from the God Instinct.

Isolation and separation
become the solution

for the confusion based Denial.

The only way out of the vicious circle
is to drop out
and drop into
Source,
I must go to Source
to get relief
from Guilt.

AS A BODY OF WORK

We are unwinding the place
that says we aren't good enough
We didn't do enough
we could have done it differently
We could have done it
better
We could have listened
more
We could have . . .
and we keep turning till we turn
to light.

SPIRAL UNWINDING DEPRESSION
(Track 10)

I'm so tired of feeling this way will I ever feel any different I'm so tired of feeling so tired I need help I need to feel better I don't ever get to have any fun I always have to be processing stuff I need a break err err eeee err ah ah er ah ah oooo u u uuuuu

CLOSER TO ORIGINAL SEPARATION

Pat Scott, as she lay dying ,
shared with me her very recent experiences
with Sound:
"Sound is the midwife of releasing old
tensions," she said,
"it is the midwife for releasing pain and disease.
Lack of God presence is tension.
God Presence is in the cells.
Source is right there in us."

A SHARED COLLECTIVE

These are voices of the
stored emotions
collected through
the years
of Guilt, Anguish,
Pain, Fear, and Shame
of not having
a Feminine
Source,
a Feminine Face of God.

There are many stories
Put together in these Pieces.
This is a most difficult placement of
embodiment and needs to
be given much
Grace and Compassion.

SMALL DOSES OF REMEMBERING

This is not Personal
and This does not belong
to either Gender
This is a Collective.

I have found that everybody's Body holds this feeling of betrayal.
If we have a Female God,
we feel we are betraying our Male God.
If we have a Male God,
We feel we are betraying our Female God.

Several thousand years ago, approximately 6,000
we divorced Mother and Father God
We pitted ourselves against ourselves.

GENETIC CO-DEPENDENT TALE

There is a Genetic Story, that is also generic,
    that runs through our cellular
        Systems,
            this story seems to have
an insertion in all parts
of self
    and that story tells of the
    pain of holding the separation
        of Mother and Father
           God.
    We want
        Their Relationship
            Healed in us.

The Father-God stories,
    the Father-Self stories,
      the Daddy-Loss stories
              seem
            to be all meshed
                into one.
    Not much delineation
    cellularly.

GROWING A HEART

There must become a moment
that's surely a Leap of Faith.
To become ultimately successful
one must eventually Surrender
Completely to Heart
which allows a heart to grow.

HEART PIECES

My Heart tears in my Hands
    Falls apart in pieces
        I can't find
            as they scurry
                across the
                    floors and walkways.
Traveling somewhere
            anywhere
      they run
          hollow
      but, mainly the
     pieces of my Heart
     hurry ever - so - fast
       to get away.
They seem scared, I think
            but don't really
               know
      How the pieces of my heart
       feel.
One piece feels one way
    another piece feels
      another.
One says, "I'm going with
    Father-God"
Another says, "I'm going
          with
              Mother-God"
Another piece says, "I want
         to be with Mother and
           Father God."

Oh my, the pieces are
          scattered and each
          has its own force,
its own timing, its own place of trust,
its own place of survival,
      How will these pieces
        ever find a place
           to cooperate?

NOTHING IS PERSONAL BUT GOD

These stories are not
  of a Personal
            Mother
  a Personal
            Father

But the absence
  of a personal,
            open
  acknowledged
relationship
  with Mother-Father-
                God
                        Goddess
  Spirit
            Will
  Body
            Higher Power
(Fill in your
  own . . . Cosmology)

It has become a
  radical . . . almost
            political
  position
to acknowledge
  a personal
            relationship
                with
                essence

Please may we become Aligned Revolutionaries?

PAIN OF DENYING MOTHER GOD

Mother . . . I am here
Mother . . . You are Whole
Mother . . . I need to record your presence within this form . . .
                                    that you have always been there . . .

But . . . you were a problem
You . . . didn't feel good
You . . . complained a lot
You, you were actually pretty pitiful
You made me tired to be around you
You . . . You . . . You
Caused so much trouble
Never let well-enough alone
Always was asking for the truth
Always was asking for integration
Always was asking for Reality checks . . .
                                    from us All.

Mother . . .You're messy and sticky and muddy and cluttered and
                                    sloppy!
                        Not proper for God to see.

Oh, Mother! Please take care of Yourself . . . Will You?
Get Yourself together!
It's embarrassing being around You . . .
It's humiliating being around You . . .
Actually, I really don't have much time
                                    to be around You

Mother, why can't You be more like the Madonna, you know, Mary and
                        Saraswati and . . . other Saints?

170

Why do You have to be so needy?
Why can't You just relax with what You have?
Why do You want everything to be different?
Why do You want to cause trouble and just make everyone
        feel uncomfortable and blame You for causing
             this disturbance and dis-comfort.
Oh, why, oh, why? Can't You be satisfied with things
        the way they are?
               Why do You always want more?
Why do You have to be so dramatic?
    So intense? so obvious?

Don't You see, You're a reflection of me? . . . and the more You draw
attention to Yourself and Your suffering, people notice Me?
    The Light shines on Me . . . and,
    They start thinking I'm like You
    And, I start feeling I'm like You and,
    I'll never be free of You and Your victimized, messy,
        painful, suffering ways.

Oh, Mother . . . No one wants to hear about You, in this way.
The topic is considered inappropriate, uncomfortable, and disrupting
. . . let alone not spiritual, not positive.
        But . . . You were always complaining,
          You were always hurting
          You were always in pain,
               never felt good.
        Except, You liked Sex a lot . . .
          too much
            for a Mother.
Just can't take You anywhere!
You are always dressed to kill . . .
or shabbily attired!

And never know what's going to come out
        of your mouth
Some form of Truth . . .
That will only make Others squirm
      or create a giggling
  of discomfort.

Ah, Mother
    You push us to actually
        be willing to name
            that which is evil,
      to actually acknowledge
            that there are groups that
      would rather not see
            healing take place.

To acknowledge that there
    are those that only
        want healing to look
            a certain way,
      the way it has been
            for several thousands
                of years
      and that way has
            been at the
                exclusion of Mother.

We have virtually had to
    make up Mother
        as we really have
            not had much experience
    of Mother as a reality
            form of Presence.

But, Mother . . . the Truth is that You have always been here . . . Present.
        Just unacknowledged,
        hidden and used for the good
        of greedy-minded people.
So the pain has been the mis-interpretation of You.
The pain has been in having to deny your Presence.
The pain has been having to pretend we are not whole.
The pain has been having to pretend we were whole without
You.
The pain has been to pretend You were other than You are.
The pain has been You watching Me pretend.
The pain has been You watching Me deny You.

WHINING TO GOD

OH, mother,
OH, father!
Can you hear my call
can you feel my quest
can you seek my rest
from all of my best?

Do you hear me
So I speak thee
Do I own my Will
to know what is ill
and now, that I am
and now, that I am
and now, that I can
and now, that I blend
Will I be all?

I hear you, my daughter
you whine still
you mime still
are you still . . .
waiting to have it all?

When will you just bend
and wind and entwine:

I have told you that you are well

You only need this:
to not dwell
any longer in the till
of your mind

SPIRAL OF LOVING KINDNESS
(Track 10)

Being kindness to all self-compassion to all kindness loving myself for compassion Loving kindness o ah o o u ah ou ah ou ah ou ah ou ah ou ah o u ah o u ah u u u u u u m m m m m m m m m m m m m m u u u u u u n n o no no no no n u u u o o o o o o o ah o o u ah o ah o ah

175

IT'S YOUR TURN

Grace us, Father
Grace us, Mother
    Grace us with your mercy
    Grace us.

Grace Us?
    Us?
It's your turn, not mine
    It's your turn, not mine . . .

We've had our time . . .

I've had plenty of time to be
    Lost and drugged

Through the ages, through the mud

It's your time
    It's your turn
    It's your burn,
        NOT MINE!

Grace yourselves
    If you've got one,
Grace yourselves,
    If you're going to get one,
Grace yourselves
    If you want one.

It's your turn to do the gracing
It's your turn
To do the burning
It's your turn to fail the Angels.

It's your turn . . . to turn
It's your turn, to turn.

Grace us! You gotta be kidding!
Grace us! You must be sitting
right now on some hard rock
Wishing you had got another spot.

Grace us! Don't you ask!
Grace us! This won't be the last
Time . . .
I tell you

IT'S YOUR TURN.

BECAUSE WE FEEL SHE CANNOT BE HEALED

Because we feel She cannot be healed
keeps Mother so difficult for us
to embrace.

Mother needs so much healing.
It is like a deep hole,
a dungeon,
a bottomless pit,
a never-ending drama and tragedy.

But mainly, we are afraid,
afraid we will fall into Her womb of despair,
Her womb of helplessness and hopelessness,
Her constant neediness.

We fear that we will succumb to Her power and
will fall into the abyss of Darkness,
swallowed up, enveloped, drowned in Her dark waters.

We don't know that by healing Her we will heal ourselves,
that by supporting our Mother we are supporting ourselves.
We can heal ourselves by being fearless,
by going into our own darkness,
by embracing our own womb of vast darkness.

All we need to do is to Love.
All we have tried to do was to hold back our Love
from ourselves, from You, Mother,
to hold back our Love until we felt more deserving,
more together,
to hold back our Love out of fear
of loving and sinking with You.

PREMISE FOR MOTHER PIECES

The "Mother stories"
    are stories I've heard
called shame
      called sin
    called guilt
      called hate
    Definitely called Pain

The Pain of having to
    admit denial
      of self
    at least half-of-self

The terror of possibly
    being found
      admitting the
        existence of
          A Mother-God

The many memories
    of terror
      and dread
    found in the tissue
      of men and women
    for having
      owned their
        inherent wisdom
    to have been forsaken
      of the EARTH and beyond
          for having
this knowledge.

THEY DON'T REMEMBER

My breasts are heavy, large, hanging low
    Been feeding babies all my life
Those babies are grown now
    and they want to date me,
                mate me
                make me
their slaves, their women
    their teacher, their students
      their competitor.
They don't remember that I was
    their mother
and I won't belong to any of those
      places, spaces, in time.

MOTHER FEELS TIRED

Mother feels tired
    Mother feels wasted
    Mother feels spent
    Mother feels . . .

Mother feels more
    Mother feels less
    Mother feels all
    When Mother feels the best.

Mother spent days
    Feeling . . .
Mother spent nights
    Feeling . . .
Mother spent her life spending
Her last spinning on you.

Mother is tired
    Mother is dead tired
    Mother is dead
to most.

Mother not giving much juice
Mother not giving no truce
Mother is spending mother-self
              forward
This we cannot refute.

Mother is bone tired
    of futile gains

When all remains
        Truth.

What does Mother feel?
    What must Mother feel?
    What is real
    What Mother feels?

You asking me?
    You asking me!
    Me! Who feels the leaf fall
    Who feels the shadow burn
    Who only yearns
    to not feel.

You asking me
    What Mother feels?
    What is real
What is real?
    What is real
    What is real?!!

You asking me?
    Do you know that I don't
    know what I feel?
    Do you know that I don't
    know what is real?
    Do you know that I don't
    know that I don't know
    that I don't know
    what Mother feels?

A MOTHER-LESS MOTHER

I want to comfort you
and I push you away

I want to cuddle with you
and I push you away

I want to make it better for you
and I feel sorry for me

I want you to love yourself
and I criticize you

I want you to feel loved
and I yell at you

I want you to feel secure
and I am bored with being with you

Mother is tired
Mother is scared
Mother is bored
Mother is stressed
Mother is wanted
Mother is busy

Mother is not ready
to be here
Mother is unavailable
Mother is crazy
Mother is depressed
Mother is too alone to be at home
Mother is tired of being criticized
Mother is tired of taking all the pulls
and the yanks and the kicks
Mother is tired of not being appreciated
Mother is tired of depreciating.

EXPRESSED PAIN OF DENYING MOTHER AS GOD
BLUEPRINT
MOTHER RECEIVED

Oh, Mother, it has taken so long
to receive You
to believe You
to relieve You
of Us.

Of all of our fears of You
to shed all of our tears of You
to sanction the place
of rest, that lives in You.
To acknowledge Mother . . .
is to acknowledge our Wholeness
To acknowledge Mother . . .
is to let ourselves be Well
To acknowledge Mother . . .
is the Path of the Way Ahead.
To acknowledge on the same plane
at the exact degree
one without a second
position . . . as we give
Father-God
Acknowledge that there is no difference
of Honor.
To truly acknowledge there isn't
any Father-God
without Mother-God
there isn't any Father God
without Mother God

And to take this understanding to our cells
And, knowing that our healthy Wholeness
is because
we honor and acknowledge
That we are all Mother
That we are all Father
That is our wellness
That is our wholeness
And anything less
Creates our Dis-ease.

SOUNDPRINTS OF
MOTHER RECEIVED NOTES
(Track 11)

me ye la me
me ye la me
me yela me

me ye la me
me ye la me

me ye la me
me ye la me
me ye la me
me ye la me
me ye la me

me ye la me
me ye la me
me ye la me
me ye la me
me ye la me
me ye la me

me ye la me
me ye la me
me ye la me

te he le te mi la do
temeletemlado
temletemelodo
temlotemledo

A la lo no a se
Ala lo toe swee
Ala lo tow swee
Ale lo lo to Swee

Ala ho ha ha ha Sa
Ala ho ha ha ha Sa

Shree alo
Aha h le gioni

187

SPIRAL LOVING SELF
(Track 11)

FATHER-PIECES

The poems/pieces about
        Father
are varieties of ways
      I have seen
          us unravel
Generically our
      feelings of denial
Betrayal, Rejection
      That are from and of Father.

Father was never there,
      even if you had one
Father was absent
      Father wanted and had
        sex with you
Father was beaten down
      and had become invisible.

These are a lot of the stories
      I have heard through the years

Now in sounding the body for
      unraveling the Father stories
We find the daddy stories
      we unwind some more
We find the husband or lover stories
      we unwind some more
We find the male-dominate world stories
      'cause they're everywhere
        and we unwind some more

We find our inner male-female story
        and we unwind some more

We find our Father-God story
    closer to the original cause story
      possibly
        and we unwind some more.

FATHER NEED

Unwinding the holding pattern
   of feeling unloved
       denied
       betrayed
       rejected
  from Father
    is the doorway
       and pathway
       of being free
       to receive
       gold
       transformation
       rest
       cooperation

Now I am not saying that this
   particular feeling of holding
     is in everyone
I am just stating that the
   thousands of folks I have met with
     tend to have
       the bottom line feeling of
       needing and wanting
       nourishment in their
       core
         from Father

SOUNDPRINTS UNWINDING
(Track 11)

Sho no me ta lo se

Kay Kay Kay

lo ma ta me se

kay kay

lo oh se kay ehel

FATHER LOSS

I miss you, my son
I miss you, my kin
I miss you, my cherished one.

Oh, God, when did it end
When you knew you could trust me
and crawl into my arms
and that I would care for you
and bring you no harm.

When did it end, my shining one
That you started doubting your love
When did it end, my precious one
That you forgot you were a star
When did it end, my glorious son?

I miss you, my son.
I miss you, my only one.
I miss you, my glorious child
I miss you.

DEEPER INTO FATHER - LOSS

The poor little man
is crawling for his life
is crawling for his living
is crawling for his dignity
is crawling
is crawling

The poor little man is crawling
is crawling
and it's in his skin
it's in his blood
Anything it takes
to keep his head out of the mud
to keep his head
above the sand
to keep his destiny
with his bond
of denial
and distrust
of lust
of lost hopes
and dreams
there is never a way
to get his dreams

DEEPER, YET

I know that poor man
I know him well
I know you can't see him
I know you can't tell
What he might have been
What he might have been
able to tell
if he'd just had a voice
if he'd just known how
if he'd just had a chance
if he'd just been born different
if he'd just not drunk
if he'd just not been illegal
if he'd just not fought
if he'd just been able to
remember
if he'd just been white
if he'd just been black
if he'd just been right
he'd been all right.

Enough of your whining
and complaining
Enough of Blaming
Come to me Now
And let us
Go onward
together

Following the path of wellness
looks like following the path of discord

SPIRAL OF DISCORD INTO HARMONY
(Track 11)

Father . . .
We have always assumed
you were there
And, we have always Pretended
that you cared.
Even though we didn't know for sure,
except sometimes . . .
We did
And, that made it worth it all
the times . . . We didn't.

Thank you
Amen

SOUNDPRINT OF FATHER NOTES
(Track 11)

A la la ha sa ga na
   s yr yi yo - ah uh
      mmmmmmmmmmmmmmmm
esa ne no ne no ne no ne noooooooooooooooooooooo
          neeeeeeeee
          nenooooooo

   ne me yin yoya
    ne me yin yoya
     ne mi yin yoi ya
   elemenna
    elemenna
     elemenna
  ne ne ma no ma le
   ne me ma no na le
    ele en no mo - el le
no mi elle en ne ma
eooooooooooooooooo
   . . . .
    . . . .
e lo ma ha e lo o
ye yo e la ma hale
  O ma
ye lo mahali
   O - O - Ooooooooooo
ye la ma haler
  ye la ma holei
    e o u u u u u u u u u u u u u

Sound
as Food

Surrender
is
food
for all
Systems

SURRENDER IS GRACE-A BEGINNING

I surrender
I surrender
I surrender

I surrender to the past
I surrender to what is dead
I surrender to what is dying
I surrender
to the creator of all things
of all ways
of all times

I surrender to correct motion
I surrender to rightful placement
I surrender to the right use of will
in action

I surrender my heart
I surrender my body
I surrender my mind
I surrender

Surrender is of the essence
Surrender is the format
Surrender is the direction
of the position
of accepting

The form that our unraveling
spiral dictates
us to listen to
to follow still our
form of
preference.

SURRENDER IS GRACE

Surrender is when you can't do any more
to keep yourself from feeling
love
hope
mercy
Regardless of
your own
particular content

Our Central Nervous System
Body
loves the
Sound of
our own
Voice

ACCEPTANCE IS WHAT WE'RE AFTER

Sound makes you Honest
   'Cause only you know
      if you're activating
         igniting those
            in-between-notes.
Sound keeps you Honest
   'Cause only you know
      if what you're voicing
         is what you're following
           and it's not
               yet another way
   To blame or dump your
      emotional content
         or baggage
    on someone else,
         even yourself.
Sound wants you to be Honest
   'Cause then it gets to
    follow its discontent
         to a place of
           comfort.
Sound makes you Honest
   if you're willing to say
         just what's there
           and nothing more
    And go to the core
         of that particular
            arrangement.

Sound makes you Honest
   if you sound enough
      to get quiet
         enough
      so you can actually
         listen to what
            is there.

Sound will encourage you to be Honest
   if you will
      allow those
         in-between-notes
      those-what-I-
         haven't-wanted-
            to-know notes
  To move in their own
      timing and order.

Not to rush them
Not to push them
Not to try and re-arrange them
Not to hang out in them
Not to gloss over them
   Just be-in-the
      in-between notes
   of your
      Voice.

Sound asks you to be real.
   Sound wants nothing less
      Than for you to find
         the place of acceptance
           of your realness

Regardless of your opinions
    and judgments
        about how you should sound
    and what your healing should or
        could look like
    if you hadn't done or
        did already
    whatever it took.

So the Acceptance is great
    and challenging for sure
        not from a place
            of give-up

    but acceptance
      is from a place where you're going to get
      more.

Acceptance is what creates
    the pulsation of
        permission.
    To go
        to evolve
           yet further.

Acceptance is not an end.
    Acceptance is the grace
        of being in not-knowing.

Acceptance is a place where
    the mystery lives,
        where magic abides

Acceptance is a "Big Juice"
      in this system
of un-raveling
      of maturing these
      emotional/feeling
         arenas.

'Cause sound makes us Honest
    and the system that is
        listening knows
           immediately . . .
               one-without-a-Second
If you are trying to Pretend
    Trying to make noise
        Trying to do it "Right"'
    Trying to miss the Fire
        of your experience.

Creating a Space
with our Voice
for Trust and
Relaxation

embodiment starts from your feet
what a treat!

APOLLO SING

Let's sing your song
and take away the words
that were once your world

Let's sing your song
And take away the Blues
that was once your mood

Let's sing your song
to take away all the ways
that created your pain

Let's sing your song
to take away all that
isn't you
So that you
can become your words
in truth

Let's sing your song
and sound away the past
in your blood
So that you come out of the
mud
and fire yourself
free
of the Past
you called
"me"

REPETITION IMPORTANCE

Repetition helps get inside
encrustation
opaque layers.

Repetition massages and chips
away the
hardness of
the death imprint,
Denied Spirituality.

Repetition is becoming more and
more necessary as we are
losing more Repetition Sounds of
Insects and Birds.
The Sounds of the Rainforest.

These Sounds are nurturing to
our Systems. They keep us alive.
We must make these Sounds
now to feed our Systems
so that We do not
become Malnourished.

REPETITION

Repetition sounds
>of the frogs
>of the crickets
>of the humming birds' wings
>of a chattering squirrel
>of the cicadas
>are on an inherent sound-rhythm for these bodies

Over and Over and Over and Over
>and Over and Over and Over
>>and Over and Over
>>>and Over

The power of many
>>mantras
>>and prayers
>are the repetition
>>to feed
>>>to these bodies
>>>>food

Krya Cha Ta Krya Cha Ta
>>Krya Cha Ta
>>>Krya Cha Ta

Will find itself being said
>one hundred times to a body
>>before the body
>>>can find the timing
>>>>to receive

Repetition is a food
>let yourself have it
>>until you're full
>>>of yourself.

EXERCISE REPETITION ALPHABET
(Track 12)

Say the ABC's in various rhythms
AAABBBCCCDDDEEEFFF . . .

combine them with vowels and consonants .. .

AH AH AH
BAH BAH BAH

BE BE BE BE
BOBOBOBO
BUBUBUBU
BYEBYEBYE

many and any combinations
play with the letters
notice where they touch you internally,
notice the ones you like
do not like,

this is a simple and fun way to start loosening up your body
and your voice

FIRE

How would I feel if God
had been referred to as She
and Her and Goddess
and Mother
    and Womb
      and Vagina
       and my Blood
as the cleansing
      Juice
and Nectar
  for all to see
    and touch
and taste
As the glorious wellspring
that holds the many
dimensions of Earth
     together?

MOTHER SING

Mother sing
    Mother sing
        Mother sing your song to me

Mother song
    Let Her sing for you
Mother's song
    Just goes on and on

Mother sing to me
    Mother sing through me
        Mother sing within me

I will sing to you mother's song
    I will listen to you
        in time
            and rhythm of your song

Your song of nurture
    your song of struggle
        your song of Blues
            Your song of hues
                your song of lust
                    your song of life

Your song of knowing how to live
    your song of knowing how to die
    your song of knowing when to move
    your song of knowing when to go
your song of knowing how to know
    when to listen and when to be known

I'll sing to you
    I'll sing for you
I'll be a singer with you

You sing to your creator
and I'll sing to mine
We'll blossom and flower
and remember the times
when life was so simple
and we knew our way
We'll remember enough
to follow the creation
of what are the new forms
and what are the new ways

ENTERING

This is what is now
    to enter within
        deeper into Mother
        deeper into Father
        deeper into heart
        deeper into will

Deeper into will
    Deeper into will
        Deeper into will
        Deeper into will

We are deeper into will
    we are deeper into will
    we are deeper into will

We cannot be made still
    we cannot be made still
        we cannot deny will
    we cannot not identify
    we cannot not identify how the denial
        KILLS

I AM HERE FOR YOU, NOW!

Come to me now, Child!
    Come to me now . . . !
    You've been led astray
        By voices and Light
            that has made
                me appear
                    Gray . . .

Cold to the touch
    uncaring to the mind

This is the Past
    You must let go
    of that Past
    At Last

Come to me Now
    I am your Father

Come to me now
    Do Not Look Back

You've had your Time
    of feeling Betrayed
        Rejected
        Maimed
    by my Light

You've had your time
    to create Reasons
        of why you were Right.

But, Now come to me Now !
Let yourself Receive me
Let yourself know me
Now
Let my Blue flame mend
your Gap of sorrow

Let my Blues be felt
in your form
Let my Golden Light
melt your stories
of the Past.

Let the Past Be So
So let it Be.

Now, come to me.

I Am Here for you
This is not Before Now
This is Now Before
Come to me
This is Your Father
this is Now.

MOTHER SPEAKS

The Mother tells me to forgive all
    that have assaulted Her.
The Mother tells me that it is Her job
    to correct the placement of knowledge,
                not mine.

The Mother tells me to release my resentment,
    to release my rage . . .
    that I am to be an example of Her Mercy,
    not to portray Her as being unable to heal.

The Mother tells me to remove Her from the
            victims' roster . . .
      to remove Her from the survivor list.

Mother God   (Track 12)
Father God
Mother God
Father God
Mother God
Father God
        Mother God
                Father God
                        Mother God
                                Father God
                                        Mother God
                                        Father God
                                Mother God
                        Father God
                Mother God
                Father God
                Mother God
        Father God
    Mother God
        Father God
                Mother God
                        Father God
                                Mother God
                        Father God
                                Mother God
                                        Fa-r G-d
                                                Ma-r G-d
                                                    Fa-r Fa-r
                                                        Ma-r
Ma-r Ma-r
    Famar
        Famar
            FaMaFaMafamafama
                famafamafama
                    famaahahahahaha
                        ahahhahhaahaha
                            mmmmmmmmm
                                ahmahmahmahmahm

SINGING A HEART

Our prayers, Mantras
    and Incantations
    Create Room for
      Acceptance
    Create Room to
      Grow a Heart

Our Prayer of
      Movement
    helps dissolve
      our Judgments
    for having the need
      to Grow
        A Heart

The Rhythms of Our Prayers, Mantras
    and Incantations
      are Food
        For
          Transformation

RESTING ASSURED

Quietly rest, my Beloved.
So much does the outer world disrupt you,
so much is confusion in that world,
that more than all else
you need a time for simple resting in My Love
and a drinking in of My Peace.
Come close that I may enfold you.
Rest, Assured.
Put aside all thought of confusion and distress
and allow My divine plan to flow through you
and all your affairs.

So step aside for a few moments
from that world so full of distress,
and resting in My Presence
you shall be able to fulfill your destiny
and the service you were meant to do.

From *In His Presence*
By Eva Dell Werber
(DeVorss Publications, 1948)

REST BLUEPRINT 1

What do I mean when I say
"Rest"

What do I intend when I say
"Rest"

What do I mean?
I'll tell you.

I mean you sit for awhile
and let yourself feel,

You sit for awhile
and let yourself season
a few . . .
to know what the movement
looks like
what is the rhythm
of the tides
how often do they come
and how often do they
flow.

I mean . . .
you sit a moment
to know . . .
if you're even interested
before you turn your head . . .
in another direction . . .
you wait a moment to witness . . .
to pause.

TRUSTING REST EXERCISE

Rest is of utmost importance.
Rest is an essential ingredient for
digesting
assimilating.

Trust that the bed supports you
Trust that the earth supports you
That every muscle and organ and
thought and
feeling
can be received
by your bed,
by your chair
by your pelvis
by your feet.

Rest is the prerequisite to
learning and practicing
receiving.
Rest is what allows the muscles
and tissues and bones to
find the comfort to feel
what's under them
what's between them.

Rest is what begins the tracking
and listening to
our own particular rhythms
of blood pulsating
of our many systems assisting each other
in such a wide arrangement of order.

PRAYER RITUAL FOR POSITIONING TO PRAY / SPEAKING THE UNSPOKEN

I Accept that Life has been hard
I Accept that Life has felt hopeless
I Accept that I have felt despair
I Accept that I have not wanted to be here.

I Accept that I have felt like I couldn't make it.
I Accept that I have had great Judgment about whether
          or not I made it.
I Accept that I have had much judgment about how my life
          has looked.
I Accept that I have had much judgment about every
          way that I have felt.
I Accept that I have felt terror that I would never know
          anything but terror.
I Accept that I couldn't feel any light at times.
I Accept that I had plenty of judgment of not being able
          to feel or receive light.
I Accept that I judged myself as not being good enough,
          evolved enough, because of how my
          Life felt.
I Accept that I judged myself for giving myself too much
          slack, too much feeling.
I Accept that I judged myself for not giving myself
          enough slack
          or time to feel.
I Accept that I have been all these ways and that Life has not missed me . . .
          that life touched me.
I Accept that I had great judgment towards others for
          not having been as touched as me.
I Accept that I was angry for my friends dying and me
          having to stay.
I Accept that I didn't want to be here.

I Accept that I was afraid to have to be here,
        as I didn't want to feel the pain of living.
I Forgive myself for all the Judgments I have made
        about how I feel.
I Forgive myself for any memories that say I should feel
        or be different from what I am.
I Forgive myself for wanting to die.
I Forgive myself for any judgments I have about dying.
I Forgive myself for the judgments I have about Living.
I Forgive myself for any belief system I have about
        dying.
I Forgive myself for all my judgments about judgments.
I Forgive myself for being hard on myself.
I Forgive myself for any belief system that still believes
        my Life should be different than it is.
I Forgive myself for any belief system that still believes
        that I need to be a certain way
            to receive light.
I Forgive myself for any belief system that says I need to be
        a certain way to share the light.
I Forgive myself for any belief systems that still feel that
        certain ways of being are not
            acceptable for light.
I Forgive myself for trying to control how much light I
        receive and share.

And, I ask my Higher Power, Spirit,
        that which is of infinite Wisdom,
To release that which I have touched now.

I turn the layers that have been addressed
        over to Spirit.
Thy will, not mine.

I ask Forgiveness for trying to manipulate my own Life.

SPIRAL ACCEPTANCE, FORGIVENESS COMPASSION
FOR OUR HUMANNESS
(Track 12)

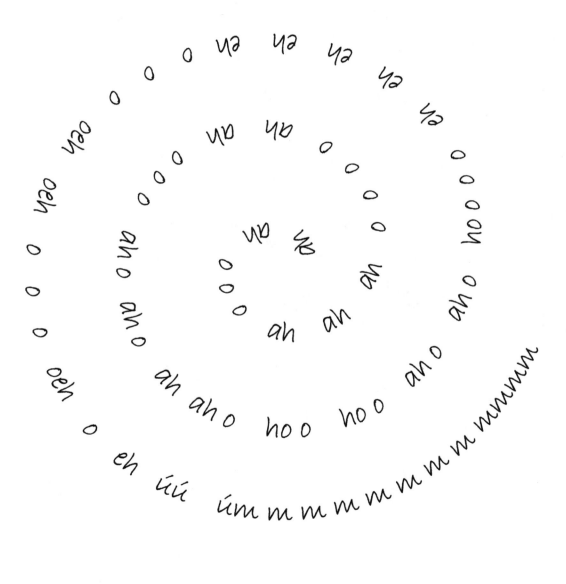

PRAYER OF NOT BEING ALONE

I am thankful for all Peoples that want to wake up
   from the amnesia,
      from the paralysis of Denial.

I am thankful for all Peoples that crave
   the right to be real.

I am thankful for all Peoples who walk their path
   as consciously as they are able.

I am thankful for all Peoples that are moving
   within a form of self-awareness and self-analysis.

I am thankful for this life.
I am thankful for this body.

We must always go to the Cause
We can release the pain, but it will not make any difference if
We do not go to the cause.

SOUNDPRINT PRAYER
(TRACK 13)

Ish was o na bo
on da bo
on da behe
on da be

Ish was o ne bo
ma lo da bo

ma da behe
behe ma da lo

E O U AH

E O U AH

E eH O U AH

Be he Ah O U

Bhe Ah OU
BHE AH OU EH AH

Ou eh Ah
Ou eh ah
lo Behe

AH EH OH

GOLD-AH

I love myself, with all my heart and soul.
And as I love myself . . .
I am loved wherever I go

GREEN-EH
Acceptance and cooperation

GOLD
Transformation

BLUE-OH

I am love

Love I share

Love I am

I accept All the Qualities

that I see in You

As Qualities that

I have in myself

(Elias DeMohan)

SING A HEART

I want to sing you a Heart Song
   I want to sing you a Heart Song
   I want to sing you a Heart
         Song
      Sing a Heart
      as we birth
        a Heart
           Song
           Sing
        a Heart
           Song
        of you
        to you
        to sing
           your Heart
              is a song
              of love

I want you to sing your Heart
        to life
      to bring your
        Heart
        to life
      to sing your
        Heart
        it's a
        Love Song

Sung for a Dear Friend and Teacher who had suffered a terrible accident. This came from her body while she lay in and out of consciousness.

THE SH . . . SH . . .
SOUNDS

Came to me many
years ago . . .

    I noticed that when I would SH . . . SH . . . SH over a Body,
        the Superficial tissue started Relaxing,
        the musculature started acting comforted.
        SH . . . SH . . . SHU . . . SH . . . SHU . . .
            SH. . . SH. . . SH . . .
            SHUSH . . .
And, appreciating that people have been holding
and cradling babies in all parts of this world and
in all languages, saying,
        shush, sh . . . shh . . .
            now, not to shut the child up,
        but, to quiet the child,
        to relax the child, to soothe . . .

Hush, now, Baby, you're all right with the World,
              Shu . . . Shu . . . Shu . . .

Sh . . . Sh SHuuuuu
  She She ShSh
    Shhhhhhhh
       Shhhhhhh
Shhhhhhhhh
       Shhhhhh
Shhhhhhh
Shuuush
sh . . . sh . . .shush

SOUNDPRINT FOR GRATITUDE PRAYER
(Track 13)

she kaink ka la so sa

she kainka lasosa

Sha kauika lasosa
Sho kauika laso

Me si mi alosa
Me si me alo
Me Si Mi alosa
Kalasalosa

Sha Nokekolosamo
Ka lo so mo kolo
Ke lo sa mo ka lo sa
Sho no kela somo

Shivakaloma
Shevakaloma
shevakalomoso
shi vokaloiho

Mo So la ti do ma
mo si la ti do
mo sa la ti do ma
kalatino so

I give you this day
I give you my ways
I give you my heart
of all my ancient ways
I give you my love
I give you my word
to honor your knowing
I surrender to this position
Gratefully . . . full

CELL-COOPERATION

Cell cooperation is what we're after.
          This is a great challenge
                    Since we know
                              how difficult it can be to
                                        get one body part to
                                                  cooperate with another.
          One mate to cooperate with another
                    One person in relationship with another
                              to agree
                    to participate at the same time
                              about any given task
                    is a feat
                    most of us treat
                    as a divine intervention,
                              to say the least.
Especially if we believe that cooperation means
          you should agree to be
                    just like me
Or that my right side should see
          that it should be
                    just like my left side
Even though we say that we know
          that the hemispheres of the brain
                    have almost totally
                              different refrains
                              and performances
                              and rhythms
                              and intentions
                                        than each other.

Then why, if I please to ask you to agree
               that to follow the spiral of your dis-ease
          is going to seem different at every degree
               and turn
               and move you make
               to find the particular geometry
That mates them, that matches them
          to a place of fate.
This place of fate gives them the permission
                    to be
          just exactly as they are
and by your acceptance of their
          diversity
               you create the star
          that awakens inside you
          the love for you that you always knew
               and hoped for.
So we have to talk to these cells.
We have to tap and touch our bodies and say
               wake up
               hello
               I need your attention
I need all of you present
I need all of your attention
          as I have a big intention
          and that is
               to get to know you
and, this is an everyday affair
          to want to know our own
following our own path creates
          inner cooperation.

THE ART OF RECEIVING LOVE

The Art of Receiving Love
is the form for touching health,
is the way of going toward wellness,
is the impetus to Resonate
  The Wellness that lies
    within us.

 The Art of Receiving
   engages the Art of Responding
 As we lay ourselves into
    the Body of Mother
 to Receive the
    Light and love
      that is giving

The Art of Receiving Love
 may be the most challenging
  of all Art-forms.
 How to Position to Receive
  is the ultimate Geometry
   to please
    US.
 To Receive the juices
   of love
     for ourselves
 Is the diameter of our
    openness
  is the dimension
    of our aperture

to know
that we
are available
to know us
so well

It is a softening at our core
that allows us to Bend
just slightly
to our
Give.

The Art of Receiving Love
is what you taught
You taught me with your
sacrifice
You taught me with your
courage
You taught me with your
willingness to
Will
Love
to you
in such a way
that it has
Broken your
Heart
Just enough
to let Love
have a place
to slip in
and Become
Yours . . . Forever.

The Art of Receiving Love
    is the Gift that
    Mother/Father God
        is trying to Bring
          to us
            NOW

From anyone that is around
    us that loves us
      in anyway
    allow ourselves to practice
      Receiving their love.

I know if I died right
      now . . . I would have
  given love . . .
    lots of love
      that people could
        tell about
          Report about.
  But, I want to die
    knowing that I
      Received love
That I wear love
    As a Badge
      to Mother-God to Father-God
That I was willing
  to receive the
    love
That they have had
    to hold
    for so long.

Do you know the pain
of not having your
love Received?
If you do, then
you can know
the pain
of not Receiving.

This song came from a dear friend who had just had a double mastectomy.

BEING WILLING TO BE WELL

Being willing to be well

is such an incredible challenge

How did you do it?

How did you get willing
to participate?

How did you release the romance
of leaving?

Ah, you are a brave Soul!

to be willing to stay

to be willing to reclaim
your birthright

Regardless of how you came
through the canal.

SOUNDPRINT LULLABY

SH . . . SH--SH . . . SHUSH
      SSSSSSSSSSSSSSSSSSSSSSSSS
SHSHSHSHSHSHSHSHSHSHSHSHSHSHSHSHSH

SHISHISHISHISHISHIHSIHSISSSSSSSSSSSSS

SH-SH . . . SH . . . SH . . . SH . . . SHU . . . SH0-SHSHSHSH

SHSHSHSHHHHHHSSSSSSSSSSSSSSSSSSS

SSSSSSSS

SSSSSS

     SSSSSHHHHHHHSSSSSSHHHHHHHHSSSSSHHHHHSSS
SSSSSHHHHHSSHSHSHSHSHHHHSSSSS
SHISSHISHSISHISHISHISHISHISHISHISHISHISHISHI

           SHUSHUSHUSHUSHUSHUSHUSHU

SHUSHSHUSHSHUSHSHUSHSHUSHSSSSSSSS

MMMMMMMMMMMMMMMMMMMMMMMMMMMM
MMMMMMMMMMMMMMMMM
MMMM
MMMMMMM
MMMM
        MMMM   MMMMM   MMMMM
            MMMMMMMMMMMMMMMMMMMMM

CD TRACKS

1 TAPPING THE LINEAGE

2 HUM AS FOOD
Intro to Hum
Hum as Food

3 SOUND TO GET QUIET
Intro to Whine
Spiral Whine
Chaotic Sound Exercise
Grounding Exercise

4 ACCEPTANCE
Soundprint of Brilliance and Essence
Soundprints of our Preference
Soundprints Acceptance

5 DISCERNMENT
Prayer Print for Sounding Discernment
Spiral Discernment

6 HUM AS MAGNET
Soundprints Essentials
Hum as Magnet
Spiral Mis-communication

7 BLUES IMPRINT
SoundPrints of Blues Imprint
Exercise for Touching Fear
SoundPrints Awakening want-a-be
Spiral of Compassion